the Vampire Diaries

STEFAN'S DIARIES

VOL. 3 THE CRAVING

BOOKS BY L. J. SMITH

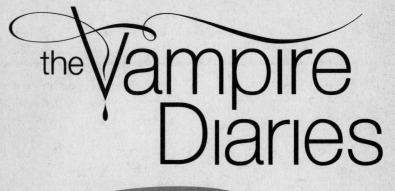

the Vampire Diaries

STEFAN'S DIARIES

VOL. 3 THE CRAVING

Based on the novels by
L. J. SMITH

and the TV series developed by
KEVIN WILLIAMSON
& JULIE PLEC

HARPER TEEN
An Imprint of HarperCollinsPublishers

HarperTeen is an imprint of HarperCollins Publishers.

Stefan's Diaries Vol. 3: The Craving

alloyentertainment
Produced by Alloy Entertainment
151 West 26th Street, New York, NY 10001
www.alloyentertainment.com

Library of Congress Cataloging-in-Publication Data is available.
ISBN 978-0-06-200395-9

Typography by Liz Dresner
11   12   13   14   15   CG/BV   10   9   8   7   6   5   4   3   2
❖
First Edition

What atonement is there for blood spilt upon the earth?

—Aeschylus

Everything has changed. My body, my desires, my appetite.

My soul.

In seventeen short years, I've born witness to more tragedy than anyone should—and been the cause of far too much of it. With me I carry the memory of my death and that of my brother. I'm haunted by the sound of our last breaths in the mossy woods of Mystic Falls, Virginia, and the image of my father's lifeless body on the floor of his study in our magnificent Veritas Estate. I still smell the charred church where the town's vampires burned. And I can almost taste the blood I took and the lives I stole out of sheer hunger and indifference after my transformation. Most clearly I see the curious dreamer of a boy I once was, and if my heart could beat, it would break for the vile creature I've become.

But though the very molecules of my being have morphed beyond recognition, the world continues to turn. Children grow older, their plump faces thinning with the passage of time. Young lovers exchange secret smiles as they discuss the weather. Parents sleep while the moon keeps watch, wake when the sun's rays nudge them from slumber. They eat, labor, and love. And always, their hearts pump with rhythmic thuds, the blood as alluring to me as a snake charmer's tune is to a cobra.

I once scoffed at the tediousness of human life, believing the Power I had made me more. Through her example, Katherine taught me that time holds no sway over vampires, so I could become divorced from it, living from moment to moment, moving from one carnal pleasure to the next with no fear of consequences. During my time in New Orleans I was heady with my new Power, my limitless strength and speed. I tore through humans as if their lives were meaningless. Every warm drop of blood made me feel alive, strong, fearless, and powerful.

It was a haze of bloodlust. I killed so many, so casually. I can't even remember the faces of my victims. Except for one.

Callie.

Her flame-red hair, her clear green eyes, the softness of her cheeks, the way she stood with her hands on her hips . . . every detail stands out in my memory with painful clarity.

It was Damon, my brother and former best friend, who dealt Callie her final blow.

In turning him into a vampire, I had taken Damon's life, so he took from me the only thing he could—my new love.

Callie made me remember what it was to be human, and what it meant to value life. Her death weighs heavily on my conscience.

Now my strength is a burden, the constant thirst for blood a curse, the promise of immortality a terrible cross to bear. Vampires are monsters, killers. I must never, ever forget that again. I must never let the monster take over. While I will forever bear the guilt of what I did to my brother—the choice I made for him—I must also avoid the dark path he is so hell-bent on following. He revels in the violence and freedom of his new life, while I can only regret it.

Before I left New Orleans, I battled the demon my brother, Damon, had become. Now, as I remake myself up North, far from anyone who's ever known me as either a human or a vampire, the only demon I have to battle is my own hunger.

I picked out a heartbeat, a single life, in the near distance.

The other noises of the city faded into the background as this one called to me. She had wandered away from her friends and left the well-worn paths.

The sun had just set over Central Park, where I'd exiled myself since arriving in New York City fourteen long days ago. The colors in this expanse of wilderness were softening, sliding toward one another, shadows blurring with the things that made them. The oranges and deep blues of the sky morphed into an inky black, while the muddy ground dimmed to a velvety sienna.

Around me, most of the world was still, paused in the breath that comes at the end of day when the guards change: Humans and their daylight companions lock their doors and creatures of the night like myself come out to hunt.

With the ring Katherine gave me I can walk in the daylight like any normal, living human. But as it's been since the beginning of time, it's easier for vampires to hunt during the uncertain hours when day slowly becomes night. Dusk confuses those who aren't equipped with the eyes and ears of a nocturnal predator.

The heartbeat I now pursued began to sound quieter . . . its owner was getting away. Desperate, I took off, forcing my body to move quickly, my feet to push off from the ground. I was weak from lack of feeding, and it was affecting my ability to hunt. Added to that, these woods weren't familiar to me. The plants and vines were as alien as the people on the cobbled streets a quarter mile away.

But a hunter transplanted is still a hunter. I leaped over a twiggy, stunted bush and avoided an icy stream, devoid of the lazy catfish I used to watch as a child, until my foot slipped on mossy stone and I crashed through the underbrush, my chase growing far louder than I intended.

The bearer of the heart I followed heard and knew her death was close. Now that she was alone and aware of her plight, she began to run in earnest.

What a spectacle I must have made: dark hair askew, skin as pale as a corpse, eyes starting to redden as the vampire in me came out. Running and leaping through the woods like a wild man, dressed in the finery Lexi, my friend in New Orleans, had given me, the white silk shirt now torn at the sleeves.

She picked up speed. But I wasn't going to lose her.

My need for blood became an ache so strong that I couldn't contain myself any longer. A sweet pain bloomed along my jaw and my fangs came out. The blood in my face grew hot as I underwent the change. My senses expanded as my Power took over, sapping my last bit of vampiric strength.

I leaped, moving at a speed beyond human and animal. With that instinct all living creatures have, the poor thing felt death closing in and began to panic, scrambling for safety under the trees. Her heart pounded out of control: thump *thump* thump *thump* thump *thump*.

The tiny human part of me might have regretted what I was about to do, but the vampire in me needed the blood.

With a final jump, I caught my prey—a large, greedy squirrel who'd left her pack to scavenge for extra food. Time slowed as I descended, ripped her neck aside, and sank my teeth into her flesh, draining her life into me one drop at a time.

I'd eaten squirrels as a human, which lessened my guilt

marginally. Back home in Mystic Falls, my brother and I would hunt in the tangled woods that surrounded our estate. Though squirrels were poor eating for most of the year, they were fat and tasted like nuts in the fall. Squirrel blood, however, was no such feast; it was rank and unpleasant. It was nourishment, nothing more—and barely that. I forced myself to keep drinking. It was a tease, a reminder of the intoxicating liquid that runs in a human's veins.

But from the moment Damon ended Callie's life, I had sworn off humans forever. I would never kill, never feed from, and never love another human. I could only bring them pain and death, even if I didn't mean to. That's what life as a vampire meant. That's what life with this new, vengeful Damon as my brother meant.

An owl hooted in the elm that towered over my head. A chipmunk skittered past my feet. My shoulders slumped as I laid the poor squirrel down on the ground. So little blood remained in its body that the wound didn't leak, the animal's legs already growing stiff with rigor mortis. I wiped the traces of blood and fur from my face and headed deeper into the park, alone with my thoughts while a city of nearly a million people buzzed around me.

Since I'd sneaked off the train two weeks earlier, I'd

been sleeping in the middle of the park in what was essen-
tially a cave. I'd taken to marking a concrete slab with the
passing of each day. Otherwise moments blended together,
meaningless, and empty. Next to the cave was a fenced-
in area where construction men had gathered the "useful"
remains of a village they had razed to make Central Park,
as well as the architectural bric-a-brac they intended to
install—carved fountains, baseless statues, lintels, thresh-
olds, and even gravestones.

I pushed past a barren branch—November's chill had
robbed nearly every tree of its leaves—and sniffed the air.
It would rain soon. I knew that both from living in plantation country and from the monster senses that constantly
gave me a thousand different pieces of information about
the world around me.

And then the breeze changed direction, and brought
with it the teasing, cloying scent of rust. There it was
again. A painful, metallic tang.

The smell of blood. *Human* blood.

I stepped into the clearing, my breath coming rapidly.
The thick stench of iron was everywhere, filling the hollow with an almost palpable fog. I scanned the area.

There was the cave where I spent my tortured nights,
tossing and turning and waiting for dawn. Just outside it
was a jumble of beams and doors stolen from knocked-
down houses and desecrated graves. Farther in the distance

there were the glowing white statues and fountains installed around the park.

And then I saw it. At the base of a statue of a regal prince was the body of a young woman, her white ball gown slowly turning a bloody red.

2

I felt the veins in my face crackle with Power. My fangs came out quickly and violently, painfully ripping through my gums. Instantly I became the hunter again: balanced on my toes, fingers flexed, ready to claw. As I made my way closer to her, all my senses became even more aroused—eyes widened to capture every shadow, nostrils flared to gather in the smells. Even my skin prickled, ready to detect the slightest change in air movement, in heat, in the minute pulses that indicated *life*. Despite my vow, my body was more than ready to slice into the soft, dying flesh and lap up her essence.

The girl was small, but not sickly or dainty. She looked to be about sixteen. Her bosom jerked as she stuggled for breath. Her hair was dark, with curls highlighted gold in the light of the rising moon. She had been wearing silk flowers and ribbons in her hair, but these, along with her tresses, had come undone, trailing out behind her head like sea foam.

Her dress had a dark red slip buoyed by frothy white cotton tulle. Where her petticoats were torn, slashes of scarlet silk showed through, matching the blood that was seeping from her chest and down her bodice. One of her doeskin gloves was white, while the other was nearly black with soaked blood, as if she had tried to stanch her wound before she'd passed out.

Thick, curly lashes fluttered as her eyes rolled beneath their lids. This was a girl who clung to life, who was fighting as hard as she could to stay awake and survive the violence that had befallen her.

My ears could easily make out her heartbeat. Despite the girl's strength and will, it was slowing, and I could count seconds between each beat.

Thud . . .

Thud . . .

Thud . . .

Thud . . .

The rest of the world was silent. It was just me, the moon, and this dying girl. Her breath was coming slower now. She would most likely be dead in mere moments, and not by my hands.

I ran my tongue over my teeth. I had done my best. I

had hunted down a squirrel—a *squirrel*—to sate my appetite. I was doing everything I could to resist the lure of my dark side, the hunger that had been slowly destroying me from within. I had refrained from using my Power.

But the smell . . .

Spicy, rusty, sweet. It made my head spin. It wasn't my fault she had been attacked. It wasn't I who had caused the pool of blood to form around her prone body. Just one little sip couldn't hurt. . . . I couldn't hurt her more than someone already had. . . .

I shivered, a delicious pain fluttering up my spine and down my body. My muscles flexed and relaxed of their own accord. I took a step closer, so close that I could reach out and touch the red substance.

Human blood would do far more than sustain me. It would fill me with warmth and Power. Nothing tasted like human blood, and nothing *felt* like it. Just a mouthful and I would be back to the vampire I'd been in New Orleans: invincible, lightning fast, strong. I'd be able to compel humans to do my bidding, I'd be able to drink away my guilt and embrace my darkness. I'd be a real vampire again.

In that moment, I forgot everything: why I was in New York, what happened in New Orleans, why I left Mystic Falls. Callie, Katherine, Damon . . . All were lost, and I was drawn mindlessly to the source of my agony and ectasy.

I knelt down in the grass. My parched lips drew back from my mouth, fangs fully exposed.

One lick. One drop. One taste. I needed it so badly. And technically, I wouldn't be killing her. *Technically*, she would die because of someone else.

Narrow streams of blood ebbed and flowed down her chest, pulsing with her heart. I leaned over, my tongue reaching forward. . . . One of her eyes fluttered open weakly, her thick lashes parting to reveal clear green eyes, eyes the color of clover and grass.

The same color eyes Callie had.

In my last memory of her, Callie was lying on the ground, dying, in a similar helpless pose. Callie had died of a knife wound in her back. Damon didn't even have the decency to let her defend herself. He stabbed her while she was distracted, telling me how much she loved me. And then, before I could feed her my own blood and save her, Damon threw me aside and drained her completely. He left her a dry, dead husk and then tried to kill me, too. Had it not been for Lexi, he would have succeeded.

With a tortured scream, I pulled my hands back from the girl and pounded the ground. I forced the bloodlust that was in my eyes and cheeks back down to the dark place from which they came.

I took a moment longer to compose myself, then pulled the girl's bodice aside to view her wound. She had been stabbed with a knife, or some other small and sharp blade. It had been shoved with near perfect precision between her breasts and into her rib cage—but had missed her heart. It was as though the attacker had *wanted* her to suffer, had wanted her to slowly bleed out rather than die immediately.

The attacker had not left the blade behind, so I placed my teeth against my wrist and tore open the skin there. The pain helped me to focus, a good, clean pain compared to that of my fangs coming out.

With incredible effort I pushed my wrist to her mouth and squeezed my fist. I had so little blood to spare—this would nearly kill me. I had no idea if it would even work now that I was feeding just on animals.

Thump-*thump*.

Pause.

Thump-*thump*.

Pause.

Her heart continued to slow.

"Come on," I pleaded, my teeth gritted in pain. "Come *on*."

The first few drops of blood hit her lips. She winced, stirring slightly. Her mouth parted, desperate.

With all my strength, I squeezed my wrist, pushing the blood out of my vein and into her mouth. When it finally hit her tongue she almost gagged.

"Drink," I ordered. "It will help. *Drink*."

She turned her head. "No," she mumbled.

Ignoring her feeble protests, I shoved my wrist against her mouth, forcing the blood into her.

She moaned, still trying not to swallow. A wind picked up around us, rustling her skirts. An earthworm dug itself deeper into the soft, moist earth, avoiding the cold air of the night.

And then she stopped fighting.

Her lips closed down on the wound in my wrist, and her soft tongue sought out the source of my blood. She began to suck.

Thump-*thump*.

Thump*thump*.

Thump thump thump.

Her hand, the one in the blood-soaked glove, came fluttering up weakly and grasped my arm, trying to draw it closer to her face. She wanted more. I understood her desire all too well, but I had no more to offer.

"That's enough," I said, feeling faint myself. I gently disengaged my arm despite her mewling cries. Her heart was beating more regularly now.

"Who are you? Where do you live?" I asked.

She whimpered and clung to me.

"Open your eyes," I ordered.

She did, once again revealing her Callie-green eyes.

"*Tell me where you live,*" I compelled her, the world spinning around me as I used the very last remaining drops of my Power.

"Fifth Avenue," she answered dreamily.

I tried not to grow impatient. "*Where on Fifth Avenue?*"

"Seventy-third Street . . . One East Seventy-third Street . . ." she whispered.

I scooped her up, a perfumed confection of silk and gauze and lace and warm, human flesh. Her curls brushed my face, tickling across my cheek and neck. Her eyes were still closed and she hung limply in my arms. Blood, either hers or mine, dripped down into the dust.

I gritted my teeth and began to run.

3

No sooner had I left the park when a hansom cab flew around the corner, followed by a policeman on horseback. I fell back into the shadows, for one breathless moment overwhelmed by the clamor.

I had thought New Orleans was big—and compared to Mystic Falls, it was. Buildings, businesses, and boats were crowded into a small, frenetic area by the Mississippi River. But it was nothing compared to Manhattan, where alabaster buildings rose high in the sky and people from Italy, Ireland, Russia, Germany—even China and Japan— walked the streets, selling their goods.

Even at night, New York City pulsated with life. Fifth Avenue was lit by a row of happy, hissing gas lanterns that gave a warm, rich glow to the cobbled street. A giggling couple bent close together, wrapping their coats more tightly around themselves as the wind whistled past. A newsboy shouted out headlines about factories on fire and corruption in city hall. Hearts beat in a frenetic cacophony, thumping and racing. The trash, the perfumes, and even just the simple smell of clean, soapy skin clung to the streets like ropy vines of kudzu back home.

After I regained my calm, I ran into the closest shadows beyond the light cast by gas lamps, the girl heavy in my arms. There was a doorman at a residency hotel up the block. As soon as he unfolded a newspaper, I staggered past him as fast as I could with my burden. Of course, if I had been at the peak of my Power, if I had been feeding on humans this whole time, it would have been nothing to compel the doorman to forget he saw anything. Better yet, I could have run straight to Seventy-third Street and been no more than a blur to the human eye.

At Sixty-eighth Street, I hid beneath a damp bush as a drunk stumbled toward us. In the close confines of the branches, there was nothing to distract me from the sweet scent of the girl's blood. I tried not to inhale, cursing the desire that made me yearn to rip her throat out. When the drunk passed, I dashed north to Sixty-ninth Street, praying no one would see me and stop to question me about the unconscious girl in my arms. But in my haste, I kicked a stone, sending it clattering louder than a gunshot down the cobbled street.

The drunk whirled around. "Hulloo?" he slurred.

I pressed myself against the limestone wall of a mansion, saying a silent prayer that he would continue on his way. The man hesitated, peering around with bleary eyes, then collapsed on to the pavement with an audible snore.

The girl let out another moan and shifted in my arms. It wouldn't be long before she woke and realized—with a loud scream, no doubt—that she was in the arms of a strange man. Steeling myself, I counted to ten. Then as if all the demons in hell were after me, I broke out into an uneven sprint, not even bothering to try to hold my charge gently. Sixty-ninth Street, Seventieth . . . A stray drop of the girl's blood spattered my cheek. A footstep echoed behind me. A horse whinnied in the distance.

Soon we were at Seventy-second Street. Just one more block and we would be there. I would drop her off at her doorstep and sprint back to the—

But One East Seventy-third Street made me pause.

The house I grew up in was enormous, built by my father with the money he had made after coming to this country from Italy. Veritas Estate had three floors, a wide, sunny porch that wrapped around the entire structure, and narrow columns that stretched high to the second story. It was equipped with every luxurious feature available during the Northern Blockade.

But *this* house—or mansion, rather—was enormous. A chateau made out of bone-white limestone, it took up nearly the entire block. Close-set windows lined every floor like watchful eyes. Wrought iron balconies, not unlike the ones that adorned Callie's house in New Orleans, hung at each level, dry brown vines clinging to the metal curlicues. There were even pointed, European-style pinnacles that boasted carved gargoyles.

How fitting that the house I had to approach was guarded by monsters.

I walked up to the giant front door, which was carved from dark wood. Depositing the girl gently on the stoop, I lifted the brass latch and knocked three times. I was about to turn on my heel to return to the park when the massive door flew open, as if it were no heavier than a garden gate. A servant stood at attention. He was tall and rail-thin, and he wore a simple black suit. We looked at each other for a moment, then at the girl on the stoop.

"Sir . . ." the butler called to an unseen figure behind him, his voice surprisingly calm. "It's Miss Sutherland . . ."

There were cries and shufflings. Almost immediately the entryway was crowded by far too many people, all of whom looked concerned.

"I found her in the park," I started.

I got no further.

Petticoats and heavy silk rustled as what seemed like half a dozen screaming women, servants, and men rushed out, fluttering around the girl like a flock of panicked geese. The smell of human blood was thick, making me light-headed. A richly dressed older woman—the mother, I assumed—immediately put a hand to her daughter's neck to feel for a heartbeat.

"Henry! Get Bridget inside!" she ordered.

The butler gently scooped her up, unflinching when the blood began to soak into his cream waistcoat. A housekeeper followed, taking orders from the still-bellowing mother, who waved maids on their various tasks.

"Winfield, send the boy to fetch a doctor! Have Gerta draw a hot bath. Get the cook to prepare a cosset and some herbed spirits! Remove her bodice immediately and unlace her corset—Sarah, go to the trunk of old linens and cut us some bandages. Lydia, send for Margaret."

The crowd filtered back through the door, one by one, except for a young boy in knickers and a cap who went dashing off, his shoes hitting the street with sharp taps as he ran into the night. It was like the house, having spewed forth a few moments of life and family and vitality, now sucked its occupants back inside to its warmth and protection.

Even if I had wished to, I would have been unable to follow after them. Humans must invite their doom in—whether they are aware of it or not. Without an invitation inside we vampires cannot enter any home, exiled from the warm hearths and friendly companion-ship that houses promise, left out in the night to simply watch.

I turned to go, already having stayed far longer than I had intended.

"Hold there, young man."

The voice was so confident, deep, and stentorian that I was pulled back as if compelled by some Power.

Standing in the doorway was a figure I surmised to be the man of the house and father of the girl I had saved. He was happily fat, with the kind of girth that causes a man to stand back on his heels. He wore expensive clothes made from wool and tweed, well tailored but in casual patterns. *Comfortable* summed up his entire demeanor, from his gin-ger muttonchops to his sparkling black eyes to the half-smile that pulled at the left side of his mouth. It seemed he had worked hard for a large portion of his life; calloused hands and a redness about his neck attested to the fact that he hadn't inherited his wealth.

For a moment the thought flashed through my head: How easy it would be to lure him out here. One more step . . . His corpulent body would provide me with enough blood to sate my hunger for days. I felt my jaw ache with the desire that would coax my fangs out, that would bring this man his death.

But despite the many temptations I'd faced tonight, I had left that life behind me.

"I was just leaving, sir. I'm glad your daughter is safe," I said, taking a step backward toward the shadows.

The man put a meaty hand on my arm, stopping me. His eyes narrowed, and though I could have killed him in an instant, I was surprised at a sudden nervous fluttering in my stomach. "What's your name, son?"

"Stefan," I answered. "Stefan Salvatore."

I realized immediately that telling him my real name like that was stupid, given the mess I had made of things in New Orleans and Mystic Falls.

"*Stefan*," he repeated, looking me up and down. "Not going to press for a reward?"

I tugged on my shirt cuffs, embarrassed at my disheveled appearance. My black pants, with my journal tucked into the back pocket, were frayed. My shirt was pulled out and hanging in loose folds around my suspenders. No hat, no tie, no waistcoat, and above all that, I was dirty and smelled faintly of the outdoors.

"No, sir. Just glad to help," I murmured.

The man was silent, as if he were having trouble processing my words. I wondered if the shock of seeing his daughter, bloodied and frail, had put him in something of a fog. Then he shook his head.

"Nonsense!" He clasped my right shoulder. "I would give anything to keep my youngest safe. Come inside. I insist! Share a cigar and let me toast your rescue of my baby girl."

He tugged me into the house, as though I were a stubborn dog on a leash. I started to protest, but fell silent the moment I stepped into the grand foyer. The dark wainscoting was cherry wood. The stained glass windows that were meant to illuminate the doorway during the day sparkled even at night, their colors jewel-like under the gaslight. A giant, formal stairway climbed to the next floor, the balustrade looking as though it had been carved from whole trunks. In my human life, I'd wished to be a scholar of architecture, and I could have gladly studied this home for hours.

But before I could fully appreciate the entryway, the man herded me through a hall and into a cozy parlor. A roaring orange fire commanded attention on the far wall. High-backed chairs with silk cushions were scattered around the room and the walls were papered in pine green. A snooker set was discreetly placed behind a couch, and cabinets of books, globes, and assorted curiosities framed high casement windows. My father, a collector of books and fine objects, would have loved this room, and my chest tightened at the realization that I would surpass my own father in life experience.

"Cigar?" he offered, pulling out a box.

"No thank you, sir," I said. The cigars were the finest quality, made from my home state's tobacco. At one time, I would have been more than happy to accept. But even the sound of a bird's beak scraping against bark almost overwhelmed my heightened senses; the thought of sucking in clouds of black smoke was unbearable.

"Hmmm. Doesn't partake." He raised a craggy eyebrow doubtfully. "You'll not bow out on some spirits, I hope?"

"No, sir. Thank you, sir."

The proper words came out of my mouth even as I paced back and forth.

"That's my boy." He prepared my drink, an apricot-colored liquid poured out of a cut crystal decanter.

"So you found my daughter in the park," he said, offering me the brandy. I couldn't help holding the sparkling glass up to the light. It would have been beautiful even without my vampire senses, scattering every stray beam like iridescent dragonflies.

I nodded at my host and took a small sip, sitting down when he motioned to a leather chair. The warm, sweet spirits poured over my tongue, both comforting me and making me feel strangely uneasy at the same time. I had gone from living in a park to sipping fine liqueur in a man-sion with a very wealthy man in the course of one short night. And at the same time that I longed to sprint back into the darkness—the loneliness that pervaded my very being begged me to linger. I had not spoken to anyone in two weeks, but here I was, invited into a veritable palace of human activity. I could sense at least a dozen servants and family members in the few rooms nearby, their heady scent indistinguishable to all but myself, and the two dogs I knew were in the kitchen.

My benefactor regarded me strangely, and I made myself pay attention.

"Yes, sir. I found her in a clearing by the remains of the old Seneca Village."

"What were you doing in the park so late at night?" he asked, fixing me with his eyes.

"Walking," I said evenly.

I braced myself for what would come next, the uncom-fortable series of questions that would assess my station in life, though my ripped clothes surely gave some indi-cation. If I were him, I would have pressed a few dollars into my hand and sped me out the door. After all, New York was not short on predators, and though he couldn't know it, probably could not even imagine it, I was the worst sort.

But his next words surprised me. "Down on your luck,

son?" he asked, his expression softening. "What was it—tossed out of your father's house? A scandal? Duel? Caught on the wrong side of the war?"

My mouth gaped open. How did he know I wasn't just some vagrant?

He seemed to guess my thought.

"Your shoes, son, show that you are obviously a gentleman, regardless of your current, eh, circumstances," he said, eyeing them. I looked at them myself—scuffed and dirty, I hadn't shined them since Louisiana. "The cut is Italian and the leather is fine. I know my leather." He tapped his own shoe, which looked to be made from crocodile. "It's how I got my start. I'm Winfield T. Sutherland, owner of Sutherland's Mercantile. Some of my neighbors made their money from oil or railroads, but I made my fortune honestly—by selling people what they needed."

The door to the study opened and a young woman I'd seen downstairs came in. She was composed and graceful, with a step that was both regal and efficient. Her cap was simple—almost like a servant's—but it accentuated her refined features. She was a rarefied version of the girl I had found in the park. Her hair was a more subtle golden shade, and her curls fell naturally in soft ringlets. Her eyelashes were as thick but longer, framing blue eyes with just a touch of gray in them.

Her cheekbones were a trifle higher and her expressions more subdued.

My human appreciation of her beauty fought with my vampire's cold appraisal of her body: healthy and young.

"The doctor has just arrived, but Mama thinks she will be fine," the girl said calmly. "The wound is not as deep as it first seemed, and appears to be mending itself already. It is by all accounts a miracle."

I shifted in my chair, knowing that I had been the reluctant source of that "miracle."

"My daughter Lydia," Winfield introduced. "The most queenly of my three graces. That was Bridget whom you found. She's a bit . . . ah . . . tempestuous."

"She ran off by herself from a ball," Lydia said through a forced smile. "I think you might be looking for a slightly stronger word than 'tempestuous,' Papa."

I liked Lydia immediately. She had none of the joie de vivre that Callie had, but she possessed an intelligence and sense of humor that became her. I even liked her father, despite his huff and bluster. In a way, this reminded me of my own home, of my own family, back when I had one.

"You have done us a great service, Stefan," Winfield said. "And forgive me if I'm speaking out of turn, but I suspect that you don't have a proper home to return to.

Why don't you stay the night here? It is too late for you to go anywhere, and you must be exhausted."

I held up my hands. "No, I couldn't."

"Surely you must," Lydia said.

"I . . ." *Say no.* The image of Callie's green eyes rose before me, and I thought of my vow to live apart from humans. But the comforts of this beautiful house reminded me so much of the human life I'd left behind in Mystic Falls, I found it difficult to do what I knew I should.

"I insist, boy." Winfield put a meaty hand on my shoulder, forcing me out of the room. "It's the least we can offer as a thank-you. A good night's sleep and a hearty breakfast."

"That's very kind, but . . ."

"*Please,*" Lydia said, a little smile on her face. "We are ever so grateful."

"I should really—"

"Excellent!" Winfield clapped. "It's settled. We'll even have your clothes cleaned and pressed."

Like a horse being steered through a series of groomers before a race, the Sutherlands' housekeeper ushered me up several flights of steps to a back wing of the house that overlooked an east-facing alleyway. Instead of my usual hollow in the rocks by the stolen gravestones, I would sleep on a giant four-poster feather bed in a room with a roaring fire, in a house of humans that welcomed me happily and quickly as one of their own.

The vampire in me remained hungry and nervous. But that didn't prevent the human in me from savoring a taste of the life I had lost.

4

November 5, 1864

It feels like so long ago, but in reality little time has passed since my transformation, since my father killed me. It was barely a month past that Damon and I tried to save Katherine's life, and her blood saved ours. Barely a month since I was a living, warm-blooded human, who sustained himself on meals of meat and vegetables, cheese and wine— and who slept in a feather bed, with clean linen sheets.

Yet it feels like a lifetime, and by some definitions, I suppose it is.

But just as quickly as my fortunes turned after

New Orleans, leaving me to live as a vagrant in a rocky hollow in the park, here I am at a proper desk under a leaded window, a thick rug at my feet. How quickly I am slipping back into human ways!

The Sutherlands seem like a kind family. I picture tempestuous Bridget and her long-suffering older sister as mirror versions of Damon and myself. I never appreciated how harmless Damon's and my father's fights were back when they were just about horses and girls. I was always terrified one of them would say or do something that would end forever what semblance of a family we had left.

Now that my father is dead and my brother and I are . . . what we are, I realize how much more serious things can get, and how simple and easy life was before.

I shouldn't even stay here, even tonight. I should sneak out the window and flee to my place of exile. Being enfolded in the warm, living embrace of the Sutherland family for any amount of time, no matter how short, is dangerous and deceptive. It makes me feel like I could almost belong to the world of humans again. They don't realize they have welcomed a

*predator into their midst. All that would need
to happen is for me to lose control once, to slip
from my room right now and take my fill of one
of them, and their lives would be filled with
tragedy—just as mine became when Katherine
arrived on our doorstep.*

*Family has always been the most important
thing to me, and I would be lying if I didn't
admit how comforting it is to be among people
who love one another, if only for one borrowed
night. . . .*

For the first time since I'd left New Orleans, I rose with
the sun, intent to slip out of the mansion and disappear
into the morning mists before anyone came to wake me.
But it was hard to resist the pull of crisp linen sheets, the
soft mattress, the shelves of books, and the painted ceiling
of my room.

After admiring the fresco of winged cherubs above me,
I pushed off the soft covers and forced myself out of bed.
Every muscle in my body rippled under my pale skin, full of
strength and Power, but every bone in my rib cage showed.
The Sutherlands had taken my clothes to be washed but
hadn't given me a nightshirt. I enjoyed the feeling of morning sunlight on my flesh, the glowing warmth fighting with
the chill in the room. Though I'd never forgive Katherine

for turning me into a monster, I was grateful at least for her lapis lazuli ring that protected me from the sun's otherwise fatal rays.

The window was open the slightest bit, ushering a cool breeze into the room and setting the diaphanous curtains aflutter. Though temperature no longer affected me, I closed the window, locking the latch with some puzzlement. I could have sworn all the windows had been shut tight last night. Before I had time to further consider the matter, the tell-tale thump of a heartbeat sounded close by, and after a light knock, the door cracked open. Lydia stuck her head in, then immediately blushed and looked away from my nearly naked form.

"Father was afraid you might try to leave without saying good-bye. I was sent to make sure you didn't charm a maid into helping you."

"I'm hardly in a state to sneak away," I said, covering my chest with my arms. "I will need my pants to do that."

"Henry will be up shortly with your trousers, freshly pressed," she said, keeping her eyes on the ground. "In the meantime, there is a bathing room just down the hall to the right. Please feel free to refresh yourself, and then come down to breakfast."

I nodded, feeling trapped.

"And, Stefan." Lydia looked up briefly and met my eye. "I do hope you'll be able to locate a shirt as well." Then she smiled and slipped away.

When I finally came downstairs for breakfast, the entire Sutherland clan was waiting for me—even Bridget, who was alive and stuffing toast into her face like she hadn't eaten in a fortnight. Except for a slight paleness to her complexion, it was impossible to tell that she'd nearly died the night before.

Everyone turned and gasped as I approached. Apparently, I cut a different figure from the hero in shirtsleeves the night before. With freshly polished fine Italian shoes, neat pants, a new clean shirt, and a borrowed jacket Winfield had sent up for me, I was every inch the gentleman. I'd even washed my face and combed my hair back.

"Cook made you some grits, if you like," Mrs. Sutherland said, indicating a bowl of gloppy white stuff. "We don't usually indulge, but thought our Southern guest might."

"Thank you, ma'am," I said, taking the empty seat next to Bridget and eyeing the spread on the large wooden table. After my mother passed away, Damon, my father, and I made it a habit to dine casually with the men who we employed on the plantation. Breakfast was often the simple stuff of workers, hominy and biscuits, bread and syrup, rashers of bacon. What was laid out at the Winfield residence put to shame the finest restaurants in Virginia. English-style toast in delicate wire holders, five different types of jam, two kinds of bacon, johnnycakes, syrup, even freshly squeezed orange juice. The delicate plates had blue Dutch patterns, and there was more silverware than I was accustomed to seeing at a formal dinner.

Wishing I still had a human appetite—and ignoring the fire in my veins that thirsted for blood—I pretended to dig in.

"Much obliged," I said.

"So this is my little sister's savior," said the one woman in the room I didn't know.

"Allow me to introduce the eldest of my daughters," Winfield said. "This is Margaret. First married. And first with grandchildren, we're hoping."

"*Papa*," Margaret admonished, before turning her attention back to me. "Pleased to meet you." Where Bridget was full of life and the plumpness of youth and Lydia was the elegant, cultivated one, Margaret had something of a practical and inquisitive good sense, an earthiness that showed in questioning blue eyes. Her hair was black and inclined to straightness.

"We were just discussing what prompted my child's

rash actions," Winfield said, bringing the conversation back to the previous night.

"I don't know *why* I ran off," Bridget pouted, drawing deeply from a cup of orange juice. The older sisters gave each other looks, but their father leaned closer, worry lines marring his forehead. "I just felt that I absolutely had to leave. So I did."

"It was foolish and dangerous," her mother reprimanded, shaking her napkin. "You could have died!"

"I am glad to see you are doing so well today," I said politely. Bridget grinned, displaying teeth that had little bits of orange pulp stuck in them.

"Yes. About that." Margaret spoke up, tapping her egg spoon on the side of her plate. "You say you found her covered in blood in the park?"

"Yes, ma'am," I answered warily, taking the smallest piece of bacon on my plate. This sister sounded more astute than the others and wasn't afraid to ask uncomfortable questions.

"There was a *lot* of blood, and Bridget's dress was torn." Margaret pressed, "Did you find it odd that there was no actual wound?"

"Uh," I stammered. My mind raced. What could I say? The blood was someone else's?

"I thought there was a knife wound last night," Mrs. Sutherland said, pursing her lips and thinking. "But it was just clotted blood, and wiping it down cleared it away."

Margaret pierced me with her eyes.

"Maybe she was afflicted with a nosebleed . . . ?" I mumbled lamely.

"So you're saying that you didn't see any attacker when you came upon my sister?" Margaret asked.

"Oh, Meggie, you and your interrogations," Winfield said. "It's a miracle that Bridge is all right. Thank goodness Stefan here found her when he did."

"Yes. Of course. Thank goodness," Margaret said. "And what were you doing in the park last night by yourself?" she continued smoothly.

"Walking," I said, same as I had answered her father the night before.

In the bright light of morning, it struck me as odd that Winfield had asked me nothing more than my name and why I'd been in the park. In times like these, and after his daughter had just suffered a great blow, it was hardly standard to accept a stranger into one's home. Then again, my father had offered refuge to Katherine when she'd arrived in Mystic Falls, playing the part of an orphan.

A nagging piece of me wondered if our story could have ended differently, if the entire Salvatore brood would still be alive, if only we'd pressed Katherine for answers about her past, rather than tiptoeing around the tragedy she'd claimed had taken her parents' lives. Of course, Katherine had Damon and me so deeply in her thrall, perhaps it would have made no difference.

Margaret leaned forward, not politely giving up the way Winfield had the night before. "You're not from around here, I take it?"

"I'm from Virginia," I answered as she opened her mouth to form the next, obvious question. In a strange way, it made me feel better to offer this family something real. Besides, soon enough I would be out of this house, out of their lives, and it wouldn't matter what they knew about me.

"Whereabouts?" she pressed.

"Mystic Falls."

"I've never heard of it."

"It's fairly small. Just one main street and some plantations."

There was some shuffling movement under the table, and I could only assume that either Bridget or Lydia was trying to give Margaret a good kick. If the blow was successful, Margaret gave no sign.

"Are you an educated man?" she continued.

"No, ma'am. I planned to study at the University of Virginia. The war put a stop to that."

"War is good for no one," Winfield said as he stabbed a piece of bacon with his fork.

"The war put a stop to much casual travel back and forth between the states," Margaret added.

"What's that to do with anything?" Bridget demanded.

"Your sister is suggesting that it's an odd time for me to come north," I explained. "But my father recently died. . . ."

"From the war?" Bridget demanded breathlessly. Lydia and Mrs. Sutherland glared at her.

"Indirectly," I answered. A war *had* claimed my father's life, a war against vampires—against me. "My town . . . it burned, and there was nothing left for me anymore."

"So you came north," Lydia said.

"To try your hand at business, maybe?" Winfield suggested hopefully.

Here was a man with three daughters, three beautiful daughters, but no sons. No one to share cigars and brandy with, no one to push and encourage and compete with in the world of business. I was both worried and amused by the gleam in his eye when he looked at me. Surely there were families with sons in Manhattan who would make for more auspicious marital alliances.

"Whatever I can do, I aim to make my way in the world on my own," I replied, taking a sip of coffee. I would have to, without Lexi or Katherine to guide me. And if I ever saw Damon again, the only thing he would guide me toward was a newly sharpened stake.

"Where are you living?" Margaret continued. "Do you have family here?"

I cleared my throat, but before I had to tell my first real lie, Bridget groaned.

"Meggie, I'm bored of this interrogation!"

A hint of a smile bloomed on Lydia's lips, and she quickly hid it behind her napkin. "What would you prefer to talk about?"

"Yourself?" Margaret said with an arched brow.

"Yes, actually!" Bridget said, looking around the table. Her eyes glowed as green as Callie's, but with her petulance on full display, she no longer reminded me of my lost love. "I still don't know *why* I ran out on the party."

Margaret rolled her eyes. Lydia shook her head.

"I mean, you should have *seen* the looks I got!" she started up, waving her knife in the air for emphasis. "Flora's dress was the worst, especially considering she's a newly married woman. And my new sash—oh no, was it ruined last night? I would hate to have it ruined! Mama! Was it on me when Stefan brought me home? We have to go back to the park and look for it!"

"How about we go back to the park *and look for the person who tried to kill you*," Margaret suggested.

"We've already had a discussion with Inspector Warren about it. He promises a thorough investigation,"

Mrs. Sutherland said. "But, Bridget, you must promise not to run off from the Chesters' ball this evening or I will be forced to stand watch over you in your bedroom."

Bridget crossed her arms over her chest with a huff.

"And neither shall you run off," Mrs. Sutherland said more pointedly to Lydia. The middle sister blushed.

"Lydia has fallen in love with an Italian count," Bridget confided, her pout evaporating as she indulged in gossip. "We all hope he asks her hand in marriage— wouldn't that be splendid? Then we'd all be like royalty, sort of, and not just rich merchants. Imagine, Lydia a countess!"

Winfield laughed nervously. "Bridget . . ."

Bridget fluttered her thick eyelashes. "It's so *wonderful* that Lydia has a suitor, much less a count. After Meggie was wed, I was afraid Mother and Papa would become traditional and not let me marry until Lydia did and who knew how long *that* was going to take."

"Lydia is . . . particular," Mrs. Sutherland said.

"Oh really, Mama," Bridget rolled her eyes. "As if anyone even had an interest before. And now she has a *count*. It's really . . . it's really not fair, you know, if you think about it . . . if I had a proper coming out . . ."

I shifted in my seat, at once embarrassed for everyone, and yet glad to be involved in something as ordinary as a family squabble. This was the first time I'd been among company since leaving Lexi in New Orleans.

"So many handsome, strange men in our lives these days," Margaret said, somewhere between whimsy and warning. "What an odd coincidence, Mr. Salvatore. Perhaps I needn't make the grand tour, after all."

"Hush now, Margaret," Winfield said.

"And actually I have *no one* to go to the Chesters' with anyhow, Mama," Bridget was continuing, actually growing red in the face as if she was trying quite hard to cry. She looked at me sidelong the entire time. "I am sure Milash won't escort me after last night. . . . I am in dire need of rescue. . . ."

Bridget widened her green eyes at her father. Winfield frowned and stroked his muttonchops thoughtfully. In that moment, Bridget seemed as powerful as a vampire, able to compel her father to her every wish. Margaret put a hand to her head as if it ached.

"Mr. Salvatore will take you," Winfield said, gesturing at me with a fork full of biscuit. "He's rescued you once; I'm sure he's a gentleman who wouldn't leave you in distress again."

All eyes were turned on me. Bridget perked up, smiling at me like a kitten just offered a bowl of cream.

I balked.

"I'm afraid I haven't the proper attire . . ." I began.

"Oh, that is solved easily enough," Mrs. Sutherland said with a knowing smile.

"Once again," Lydia murmured, too low for anyone else to hear, "we are holding poor Mr. Salvatore at our mercy. With pants."

5

At the close of breakfast, maids whisked away the Dutch china and jam, and Winfield retreated to his study, leaving me with the Sutherland women in the sunlit parlor. Bridget, Lydia, and Mrs. Sutherland had installed themselves on the brocade couch, while I perched at the edge of a green velvet chaise, pretending to gaze at an oil portrait of the family when in truth I was calculating the best way to make my escape. My last, paltry feeding seemed a distant memory, and the sweet symphony of beating hearts in this grand mansion was becoming difficult to resist.

During the meal, I'd tried several times to free myself from the Sutherlands' presence, with the aim of slipping out a window or escaping through the servants' quarters. But as though my intentions were written plainly across my forehead, I was unable to shake my company for even two minutes. When I'd excused myself to the facility, the butler had insisted upon escorting me. When I mentioned I'd enjoy lying down in my room, Mrs. Sutherland had pointed out that the couch in the parlor was the perfect place for a repose. I knew that they were grateful to me for returning Bridget to them, but I couldn't explain their acceptance of me into their home. Especially given the state I was in when I first entered it: dirty, torn clothes, disheveled, and bloody.

"Mr. Stefan," Margaret said, leaning against the column that separated the parlor from the foyer. "Are you entirely all right?"

"Fine, fine," I said. "Why do you ask?"

"You're shaking your leg so hard you're rattling the chair."

I pressed my hand to my knee to steady my leg. "I usually start my morning with a walk," I lied, pushing myself to standing. "In fact, if I may excuse myself, I think I'll take a stroll around the park."

Margaret raised a perfectly arched brow. "You certainly seem to spend a lot of time in the park."

"I consider it my second home," I said with a wry smile, picturing my cave with its cadre of statues. "I've always found nature comforting."

"What a lovely idea!" Mrs. Sutherland said, clasping

her hands together. "Would you mind if we joined you? It's a beautiful day, and we could all use some fresh air."

"Mama, I think it would be best if I rested instead," Bridget said, putting a hand to her very healthy-looking brow.

"You mean, stay in and receive visitors all day so you can tell them about your adventures," Margaret said, shaking her head. "I'm afraid I shall have to beg off, too, Mother. I've things to attend to at home, now that it appears my sister is fine—and my husband misses me."

"I can't imagine why," Bridget muttered uncharitably.

Lydia shot her youngest sister a look and lightly slapped her arm. Mrs. Sutherland ignored the sisterly sniping, shaking out a light cloak and wrapping it around her shoulders. "Come with us, Mr. Salvatore. We shall make a fine party of three."

Resisting the urge to shout in frustration—what would it take to leave this family's clutches?—I forced a smile on my face and held out my arm to Mrs. Sutherland.

The second we stepped outside the massive front door, the sun assaulted my eyes. It was a bright, lemony yellow and the sky a perfect blue. For early November up north, it was a remarkably mild day. If not for the sun's low angle in relation to the earth, it would have been easy to mistake it for a brisk spring morning.

We headed south, then crossed at Sixty-sixth Street

and walked through the wrought iron gates of the park. Despite the events of the night before, neither Lydia nor Mrs. Sutherland showed any hesitation or fear. I suppose they felt safe enough in my presence. I took a deep breath of the morning air, which seemed so clear and pure after the events of the previous night. It was as though, with the rising sun, the entire world had been washed clean. Seed heads bobbed at the ends of long grasses and flowers opened toward the sky, taking in the last bright sun of the year. The droplets of dew had already dispersed from the previous night.

We were not the only ones out to enjoy the day. The park was packed with families and strolling couples. I was struck once again with how different the North was. Yankee women wore bright colors, such as we hadn't seen in the South for years—scarlets, brilliant yellows, bold, sky blues in silk and velvet and expensive cloths like European lace, delicate stockings, tiny leather boots.

Even nature here was different. Northern trees were round, quaint, elliptical maples where our lush oaks spread out, soaking up the sun to the farthest tips of their branches. The pines were spiky and blue, not the tall, soft, grand ones the soft Southern breeze whispers around.

Mrs. Sutherland and Lydia prattled on about the weather, but they had lost my attention, for at that moment a squirrel crossed our path. A sudden darkness overcame me, as if one of the few clouds in the sky had momentarily passed in front of the sun. My predator instincts awoke. There was nothing delectable about its beady eyes or bushy tail, but in a flash I could taste it—the blood of yesterday. It invaded my nostrils and tickled my throat with desire.

"Please excuse me—I—I believe I see someone I know." I made my trivial excuse as I dashed off, promising to return in a moment, though I had no intention of doing so. I could feel Lydia and Mrs. Sutherland's eyes follow me curiously as I disappeared behind a thicket of bushes.

There sat my prey, as innocent as Bridget had likely looked to her attacker last night. It eyed me as I approached, but did not make a move. In a flash I was upon it, and it was over even more quickly. As I felt the blood seep into me—a paltry feeding, but a feeding nonetheless—I leaned against the tree trunk, awash in exhausted relief. It had not been apparent until just now how edgy I had been, every moment afraid of my own hunger. Afraid of the stirrings inside of me, and how they might control me at any instant.

My relief was so great that I didn't even hear Lydia approach, ruining my chance of escape.

"Stefan?" she said, looking around, no doubt curious to meet the person I had run off to greet.

"It turns out that I was mistaken after all," I mumbled, reluctantly rejoining Lydia and her mother on the path.

They fell back into polite conversation, while I kicked along silently next to them, berating myself for my slowed reflexes. What was wrong with me? I was a vampire. Removing myself from the Sutherlands' presence should have been no hard task, even in my weakened state. An unpleasant thought rattled at the back of my mind, an alternate explanation, that I was still with this family because I *wanted* to be.

"Mr. Salvatore, you're awfully quiet," Mrs. Sutherland observed. I stole a glance at Lydia, who gave me a smile, clearly acknowledging that her mother did not deal in subtlety.

"Forgive me. It's been a while since I've been in the midst of people," I admitted as we turned on to the bridle path.

Mrs. Sutherland squeezed my hand. If she noticed its icy pallor, she must have taken it for a chill. "Since you lost your father?" she asked gently.

I nodded. That explanation was easier than the truth.

"I lost a brother in the battle with Mexico," Mrs. Sutherland confided, as we passed a little girl and her father walking a long-haired dachshund. "We were the closest of nine brothers and sisters. Despite our numbers, none of my siblings could ever replace him in my heart."

"Uncle Isaiah," Lydia murmured. "I barely remember him. But he was always kind."

"I'm sorry to hear that. I did not mean to turn this outing into a sad affair," I apologized.

"Remembering and mourning needn't always be sad," Mrs. Sutherland pointed out. "It is simply . . . what it is. Keeping their lives present in our own."

Her words cast a true light through all the confusing thoughts that had been clouding my mind of late: how to remain in touch with my human side even as I embraced becoming a vampire, how to not lose my soul. Keeping the past present was paramount. Just as my memory of Callie kept me from attacking Bridget, my connection to my family, to the life that had once been mine, would help me keep my humanity.

Though she didn't resemble my own mother at all, for one instant, with the sunlight shining down through her cap and illuminating her graying hair, her sharp blue eyes softened with feeling, I suddenly felt she *could* be my mother. That, were the circumstances different, I could be happy in her home.

Oh, how I missed my mother. While my deep grief for her had abated in the years since she had died, there was a dull ache that was never absent from my heart. How much of the tragedy that engulfed our lives could have been avoided if she were still alive?

I missed my father, too. Up until the moment I killed him, I respected and loved him. I had wanted to follow in

his footsteps, to take on the family estate, to please him as
much as possible. My deepest wish had been that he could
respect and love me back.

I even missed my brother, or rather who he used to be.
Though he vowed to get revenge on me for turning him
into a vampire, in life he had been my truest companion in
the world, my playful competitor and my closest confidant.
I wondered where Damon was right now, and what harm
he might be doing. I couldn't judge his bad behavior—I'd
had my share of bloodlust after I had turned. I only hoped
his humanity would return to him as mine had.

"You are a wise woman, Mrs. Sutherland," I said,
returning the squeeze of her hand. She smiled at me.

"You're a remarkable young man," Mrs. Sutherland
noted. "If I was your mother, I should be very proud of you.
Of course, I have no sons, and only *one* son-in-law. . . ." She
sniffed.

"But, Mother, Margaret and I are each very accom-
plished, in our own way," Lydia said, ignoring the pointed
remark about son-in-laws. "She does the books for Wally.
And I am helping to form that charity for mothers who lack
a stable income."

Mrs. Sutherland cast a private smile at me, and in that
moment I dared to hope. Perhaps it was possible to stay
here, to become part of this family. It would be a dangerous game, but perhaps I could master it. I could keep my

hunger under control and take daily walks with Lydia and Mrs. Sutherland, accompanying them home for a cup of tea or a lively debate about the war with Winfield.

Lydia continued on, making her case for her own independence, her mother sighing despite her apparent pride. The sun grew warmer as we made our way west, choosing paths at random until we came upon a familiar foot trail in the middle of the park that led straight to Seneca Village. My home.

Perhaps it was my sudden distraction that caused Mrs. Sutherland to look at me so closely. "Mr. Salvatore," she said, half-concerned, half-afraid. "You have a . . . spot . . . upon your collar."

Despite the laws of decorum, Lydia reached for it then, brushing a finger gently near my neck. I shuddered in excitement and fear at her closeness. When she withdrew her pointer finger, it wore a speck of blood.

I grew ashen. For this was the fact of my life. Despite the pains I took to control myself, the exhaustive efforts at constant secrecy, one speck of blood was all it took to upset the balance. They would see me for who I was: a liar, a murderer, a monster.

The tinkling of Lydia's laughter broke the silence. "Just a bit of jam," she said lightly, wiping her finger on the low-hanging branch of a passing tree. "Mr. Salvatore," she teased, "I know we have made you feel very much at home, but while you are our guest, perhaps you should be more careful with your table manners."

Mrs. Sutherland began to chide her daughter, but seeing the happy relief upon my own face, she smiled as well. Soon we were all laughing gaily at Stefan Salvatore, the nighttime-hero-turned-careless-houseguest, as we made our way back into the sunlight.

6

After returning from the walk, I found myself being sewn into a brand-new suit while Mrs. Sutherland instructed the tailor on where to pin and prod me. I knew I had to leave, but I also couldn't tear myself away from Mrs. Sutherland quite yet. We spent the entire afternoon chatting about my mother and her French relatives, along with my wish to one day travel to Italy to see the Sistine Chapel.

Before I knew it, the tailor had made his final stitch, and night had arrived. Even I had to admit that my suit was fantastic. I looked like an urbane prince of industry in my pleated white shirtfront, silk top hat, and cravat. Winfield loaned me one of his pocket watches on a fob covered with a tasteful number of gold charms and gems, and I wore matching gold studs. I looked the very picture of humanity and was ashamed to be enjoying the part so thoroughly.

Bridget simpered when I offered her a hand getting up into the carriage. Her skirts were full and cumbersome, an apricot version of the white gown she wore just the night before. Cream-colored silk netting floated over everything, giving her a look somewhere between a dancer in a European painting and a giant pastry. She giggled and tripped and pretended to fall, throwing an arm around my neck.

"Save me again, kind sir," she laughed, and I reminded myself that I had only to entertain her for another couple hours. Then, no matter the affection I felt for Mrs. Sutherland, I vowed I would make good on my promise to leave the family to their lives, disappearing into the crowd of the dance and returning to my home in the park.

After a short ride, we approached another mansion of considerable size. It was solid stone, like a castle, but filled with windows. I helped Bridget from the coach and we took our places in the receiving line.

In my human life I had been to many dances, yet I was *not* prepared for a New York City ball.

There was someone to take my coat and hat—and because this wasn't Mystic Falls, where everyone of renown knew one another, I was given a ticket with a number on it to retrieve my things at the end of the evening. We approached the ballroom through a seemingly endless hallway of silver mirrors lit with candles and chandeliers, sparkling as I imagined it must have been like in Versailles. A thousand silvered reflections of Bridget and myself filled the space behind the glass.

A full orchestra of violins, cellos, horns, and flutes played in the corner, the musicians dressed in black suits. The room was filled, wall-to-wall, with dancers in the most amazing array of dress I had ever seen. The young women lifted delicate gloved hands with sparkling diamond bracelets, then twirled in gowns that ranged in color from bloodred to dusty gold. Gauzy skirts swished in time with the high-paced mazurka the orchestra played, netting, tulle, lace, and the finest silk petticoats floating like petals strewn across a lake.

If my eyes were dazzled by the sight of the dancers, the scents of the room almost overpowered the rest of my senses: expensive perfumes, huge vases of exotic flowers, sweat, and punch, and somewhere someone was bleeding from a pin left in her dress by a careless maid.

"You're supposed to fetch your lady a dance card," Lydia murmured into my ear as I stood there, stunned by the opulent and overwhelming scene before me.

"Is that . . . is that Adelina Patti?" I stuttered, pointing at a demure-looking woman standing in the corner and surrounded by admirers. "The opera singer?"

I had seen photographs of her. My father had wanted

his sons to have working knowledge of their Italian culture and heritage.

"Yes," Bridget said, rolling her eyes and stamping a pretty, satin-covered foot. "And over there is Mayor Gunther, and over there is John D. Rockefeller, and . . . can you take me to my seat now? I want to see who asks me to dance."

Lydia let out a polite cough that sounded suspiciously like a laugh.

"In the South," I whispered to her out of the corner of my mouth, "it's considered impolite to dance with your escort overmuch."

Lydia put a gloved hand to her own mouth, covering her smile. "I've heard that they still actually dance the quadrille in the South and have no parlor games at their functions. Good luck, Mr. Salvatore."

And she glided off into the crowd. Margaret gave me a tiny smirk. She was on the arm of her husband, Wally, a short fellow with a pince-nez and a serious bent. But when she whispered to him, a smile broke out and he was radiant. I felt an odd jab of jealousy. I would never know what that was like, the simple rituals of a close-knit couple.

The orchestra struck up a waltz.

Bridget stuck out her lower lip. "And me without a dance card yet."

"My lady," I said, inwardly sighing. I gave her a slight bow and offered her my hand.

Bridget was a fine dancer and it was almost pleasurable twirling her across the floor. I could forget where and who I was for the few minutes of the waltz: just a man in a tailcoat, feet flying, in a room full of beautiful people. She turned her leaf-green eyes up to me, and for one beautiful moment I could pretend she was Callie, alive and well and getting the happy ending she so desperately deserved.

The illusion came to an end the moment the music stopped.

"Lead me by the edge of the dancers," Bridget begged. "I want everyone to see us!"

She dragged me past the refreshment room, where all manner of exotic food was laid out. Delicate ices made from foreign fruit, real Vienna coffee, blancmange, tiny chocolate cakes, and glass upon crystal glass of champagne to wash it down. For the hungrier set there seemed to be every kind of fowl, from quail to goose, neatly carved into small pieces so a dancer could eat quickly and return to the floor.

Once again I wished I was hungry for normal human food. But instead I indulged in a glass of champagne.

"Hilda, *Hilda*," Bridget called out in a voice that carried well considering how crowded the space was. A beautiful girl in a rose-pink gown turned from her gentleman friend, face lighting up when she saw Bridget. Her eyes traveled up and down me with a quick flick of her eyelashes.

"This is *Stefan Salvatore*," Bridget said. "He is the one who rescued me!"

"Mademoiselle," I said with a slight bow, taking her fingertips and bringing them to my lips. Bridget gave me a look that was somewhere between jealousy and pleasure that I was so polite.

"Brooklyn Bridgey! Who's your friend?" A dapper young man with a twinkle in his eye and giant grin sidled up to us. He had a sharp nose and curly black hair; rosy dots appeared on his cheeks that made him look vaguely tubercular.

"This is *Stefan Salvatore*," Bridget told him, exactly as proudly and carefully as she had with Hilda. "He rescued me when I was overcome in the park!"

"Pleasure to meet you! Abraham Smith. You can call me Bram." He grabbed my hand and shook it hard. "That was terribly naughty of you, leaving the party unescorted like that, Bridgey." Bram shook a finger at her and she pouted.

"Brooklyn Bridgey?" I asked, my head spinning a little.

"Why, the Brooklyn Bridge is only going to be the biggest, most fantastic suspension bridge ever built!" Bram said, eyes lighting up. "No more ferries, no sir. We'll *drive* ourselves back and forth across the mighty East River!"

"Oh *look*!" Bridget squealed, pointing in a very unlady-like manner. "There's Lydia and her beau! Let's go talk to them!"

I gave Hilda and Bram a helpless salute good-bye as Bridget directed me toward her sister with an iron grip.

The Italian count was surrounded by admirers, including Lydia. I caught glimpses of him as we walked closer. His raven hair gleamed, and his black formal suit fit him perfectly. He moved with a careless grace waving his arms as he told his story. The glint of a ring shimmered on his hand.

The truth hit me only moments before he turned, as if he'd been expecting my arrival. I did my best to hide my shock when I looked into my brother's ice-blue eyes.

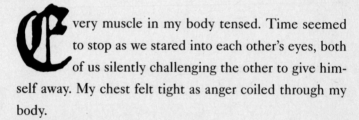

very muscle in my body tensed. Time seemed to stop as we stared into each other's eyes, both of us silently challenging the other to give himself away. My chest felt tight as anger coiled through my body.

The last time I'd seen Damon, he'd been standing over me with a stake, just after he'd killed Callie. His cheeks had been sunken, his body gaunt from his time in captivity. Now he looked like his human self, the young man who charmed everyone from barmaids to grandmothers. Clean-shaven, dressed smartly, and playing the part of an Italian count flawlessly. Acting human. He had everyone in the room fooled.

Damon raised one eyebrow at me and the twitch of a smile appeared at the corner of his mouth. To any onlooker, it would have seemed just like he was pleased to meet a new acquaintance.

I knew better. Damon was enjoying his charade and waiting to see how I reacted.

"Stefan Salvatore, may I introduce Count Damon DeSangue," Lydia said.

Damon gave a perfect bow, just barely bending at the waist.

"DeSangue . . ." I repeated.

"*Count* DeSangue," Damon corrected in good humor, affecting an Italian accent. He smiled, revealing a straight set of gleaming white teeth.

No, not here, I thought furiously. Not here in New York, not here among these innocent, well-meaning Sutherlands. Had Damon followed me here, or had he arrived first? He had been here long enough to attach himself to poor Lydia. And long enough to trick all of New York society. Is it possible that, in this teeming city, we both managed to become involved with the Sutherland family completely by coincidence?

Damon was regarding me now, although the icy twinkle of sardonic humor was never far from his eyes, as if he guessed at what I was thinking.

"Stefan, Damon—I just *know* you two are going to be like brothers," Bridget gushed to me.

"Well then," Damon said, a smirk pulling the corner

of his mouth. "Hello, brother! And where are you from, *Stefan*?"

"Virginia," I answered shortly.

"Oh really? Because I was recently in New Orleans and could have sworn I met a gentleman who looked just like you. Have you been there?"

Lydia leaned in closer, her eyes bright with pride. Bridget nodded eagerly at every word Damon said. Even Bram and Hilda looked entranced. I gripped my champagne glass so tightly I was surprised it didn't shatter. "No. I can't say I've ever been."

The happy tinkle of silverware from the refreshment table suddenly rose to the foreground. Hundreds of people, hundreds of blades, and one very angry, unpredictable brother before me.

"Interesting," he said. "Well, perhaps we will go back there, together. I hear they have a magnificent circus."

The orchestra began to play again, another fast-paced dance. But that was noise in the background. The ball and its participants faded away. Right now, Damon and I had our eyes locked on each other.

"*If you even try something*," I said low enough that only he could hear, squaring my shoulders and unconsciously tensing for a fight.

"*Don't think you can best me*," Damon said, rolling to the balls of his feet.

The group of people we were with looked back and forth at us, clearly aware that *something* was going on, but unsure what exactly.

"I'm feeling a bit thirsty," I finally said aloud, not moving my eyes from his, trying to think of how to get Damon away from my new friends. "Care to join me for a drink?"

"Smashing, I'd love one," said Bram eagerly, hoping to break the tension.

"*Love* to," Damon said, mocking Bram's tone. "But duty—and the mazurka—calls." He turned to Hilda and bowed. "May I?"

"Oh, I'd love to, but Bram . . ." She started to hold up the dance card that hung around her wrist from a pink ribbon. Then her eyes widened, dilating, and she was staring—but no longer at the card. I looked at Damon. He was also staring, *compelling* her. Showing off, in front of everyone—in front of me—just how powerful he was.

He was sending me a message.

"Oh, he won't mind," Hilda decided and took Damon's arm. He led her off, smiling back at me. The tips of his fangs glittered.

"I wish I had his charm," Bram said a little wistfully. "He's got all you ladies wrapped around his finger."

Lydia blushed prettily. She did not look after Hilda with a worried expression. She had the calm confidence of someone who knew exactly where her lover stood in his relation to her. Damon had no doubt compelled her to act as such. He had amassed a considerable amount of Power, very quickly.

"Where exactly did you two meet?" I asked, trying to sound casual.

"Oh, it was *so romantic*," Bridget answered quickly. "Almost as romantic as you finding me, helpless, in the park. . . ."

"Let your sister speak, Bridgey," Bram interrupted.

Lydia smiled, all of her studied politeness and mannered behavior melting away. "It really *was* a bit like a fairy tale. It was raining, a sudden downpour. I remember very particularly that the sun had been shining just moments earlier. Unprepared for the change of weather, Mother and I became soaked. My new hat was ruined, and all my packages were dripping wet. I swear a dozen carriages must have passed us by without stopping. And then—one of them paused, and the door opened, and there *he* was, extending his hand to me."

Her eyes grew soft. "He offered to give up his seat, but we got in with him. . . ."

Bram made *tsk-tsk*ing noises; Lydia smiled, shrugging prettily.

"I know, I know . . . 'taking a ride with a strange man.' Very bad of us. But he was so polite, and charming . . . and we had such a lovely ride . . . and then the sun came out and we hardly noticed. . . ."

My mind raced. Had Damon compelled every carriage driver in Manhattan to avoid Lydia and her mother? Was it even possible to compel that many people at once? And what about the rain? Had that been luck . . . or something else entirely? Damon wasn't capable of compelling the *weather*. If that were a power available to vampires, I would have heard of it from Lexi or even Katherine. Right?

I studied Lydia. She wore a simple, narrow ribbon around her neck with a single pearl dangling from the front. The skin there was smooth, unblemished—and unbitten. If Damon wasn't feeding on Lydia, then what did he want from her?

"Someone said something about being thirsty . . . ?" Bram said hopefully, rubbing his hands together. "I have a terrible desire for more champagne."

"Yes, thirst is a terrible thing," I said, "but you'll have to excuse me." Then I turned and cut my way through the merrily dancing crowd, determined to search out my brother before he had the chance to slit anyone's throat.

I found Damon dancing with Hilda, ushering her around the dance floor with the lightest touch. Wherever his fingers touched she bent, curling into him a trifle more than was acceptable and falling against him more than was necessary. Other girls looked on enviously, clearly hoping to dance with him next. He pretended to devote all his attention to the poor girl, but glanced up just long enough to shoot me a dazzling smile.

I waited impatiently for the dance to end, wishing I could compel the musicians to stop. But whatever Damon's powers of compulsion, mine were severely lacking thanks to my meager diet.

As soon as the last beat was played, I marched up to my brother.

"Oh, I'm sorry, did you want to . . . ?" he asked, innocently, indicating Hilda. "Because I'm sure she *will*. If you'd *like* her to."

Hilda studied her dance card, the picture of confusion.

"Let's go get a drink," I said, taking him by the elbow.

"Exactly what I was thinking," he agreed, mockseriously. He snapped his fingers, as if at a dog. "Hilda . . . ?"

"Leave her alone," I ordered.

Damon rolled his eyes. "Fine. A waiter will do just as well." But he allowed me to place an iron grip on his arm and guide him through the crowd, past the refreshment room, through a library and into a poorly lit study.

"What the hell are you doing here?" I demanded the moment we were alone.

"*Trying* to enjoy myself," Damon said, throwing his hands up in mock exasperation. He dropped his accent immediately. "Did you see the spread? The salmon's from Scotland. And Adelina Patti is here, too—Father would have just *died*. Oh wait." He snapped his fingers. "He *did* die. You murdered him, in fact."

"Only after he tried to kill us," I pointed out, clenching my fists.

"Correction: after he succeeded in shooting both of us. We're dead, brother." Damon grinned at me.

He was circling me. Casually, as if he didn't mean to, as if he was just walking around idly, making conversation while admiring the decor. It reminded me of how he'd paced the ring at the circus back in New Orleans, when Gallagher had forced him to fight the mountain lion. Damon picked up a small statuette and turned it over in his hands, but his eyes stayed locked on mine. I squared my shoulders, feeling the predator's response as he challenged my personal space.

"I'm asking you again, Damon: What are you doing here?"

"Same thing as you, brother. Starting a new life, far from home, and war, and tragedy, and all of those other things immigrants like us are escaping. New York is where the action is. I figured if it's good enough for my brother, it's good enough for me, too."

"So you did follow me," I said. "How?"

"You stink," Damon said. "Don't act surprised! It's not just you. Everyone stinks. We're hunters, Stefan. About halfway up the coast, it wasn't hard to figure out where you decided to go after New Orleans. I just made sure I got here first. There isn't a train yet that can beat me on a horse. Well, several horses. A couple of them died of exhaustion. Like your poor, poor Mezzanotte."

"Why, Damon?" I said, ignoring his casual cruelty. "Why follow me here?"

Damon's eyes narrowed and a flash of rage shot through them, exploding from the hidden depths of his soul.

"I told you I was going to torment you for the eternity you blessed me with, Stefan. Did you think I would break my promise so quickly?"

I was used to Damon's fits of pique. His anger had always been like a summer storm, quick and violent, causing damage to anyone or anything nearby—and then it was over and he was buying a round at the tavern.

But this fury was new, and it was all because of me.

I averted my eyes so he couldn't see the pain and guilt written there. "What do you want with Lydia? What does she have to do with anything?"

"Ah, Lydia," Damon sighed, infusing his voice with pretend longing. "Charming, isn't she? Definitely the best catch of the three sisters. Not that Margaret doesn't have her own charms, of course, but she's a bit sarcastic for my tastes, and, well, *married*." He shook his head. "But then there's Bridget. Such a lively girl! Such verve!"

". . . *anyone seen Stefan?*" As if on cue, we could both pick out her whining, childish soprano from four rooms away.

". . . and such an *irritating* voice," Damon finished, wincing. "First thing I would do, brother, is compel her to silence. You'd be doing the world a favor."

I clenched my jaw. "You were obviously involved with the Sutherlands long before we crossed paths here."

"Oh was I?" Damon asked. He put down the small statue he had been holding and turned it this way and that on the desk, as if deciding which way it looked best. "Poor girl was getting soaked—did she tell you the story? She *loves* it. For all of her pretending to be hard-nosed, she's a weak-kneed romantic as bad as the rest of them. A sudden storm out of nowhere, a dry cab for Lydia . . . rich, rich Lydia . . . with a sheltered upbringing and open, welcoming family."

"Oh, you are a *master* of subtlety. Controlling men's fates," I said, rolling my eyes at Damon's preening.

"I *am* a master. Who do you think left Bridget for you to find?" he demanded. He stuck his face toward my own so that our noses almost touched. "Who do you think wounded her—just enough—for poor, old, predictable Stefan to find? Stefan, who's sworn off drinking from humans, who I just *knew* would rescue the damsel in distress rather than finish her off."

A cold chill crept up my spine.

"And then of course I compelled the entire family to welcome you and take you in," he finished with a careless wave of his hand, as if it had been nothing.

A sense of resignation and understanding flooded my body. Of course he had compelled the family. The Sutherlands' easy acceptance of me into their home had rankled me, and I should have realized earlier that something was hugely amiss. How did a man of Winfield's stature let a stranger, a vagrant, into his home, and never ask anything about his family or acquaintances? A man of his kind of wealth had to be careful about whom he allowed to get close. And Mrs. Sutherland—she was such a cautious mother, yet she allowed me to escort her and her daughter on a walk in the park. Though this was hardly the time, I couldn't help but wonder if her seeming affection for me had been true, or if it all had been due to Damon's Power.

"What do you want, Damon?" I asked again. Here we were, back in the thick of it, but this time I understood just how dangerous my brother was and just how far he'd go to get revenge on me.

"Nothing terrible, Stefan!" he said, grinning and stepping back, throwing his hands in the air. "But think of it! Me with Lydia wrapped around my finger. You with the adoring Bridget. . . . We'll marry the sisters and, just as you always hoped, we'll be brothers again for eternity—or at least as long as they live."

"I'm not marrying Bridget," I blurted out.

"Yes, you are," Damon said.

"No, I'm *not*," I repeated. "I'm leaving New York. Tonight."

"You are staying here and marrying Bridget," Damon said, coming to within an inch of my face, "or I will start to kill all the people in this place, one by one."

He was deadly serious, all traces of cavalier, joking, devil-may-care Damon gone. The smoldering anger was back.

"You can't do that," I growled. "Even you aren't strong enough to take down an entire ballroom."

"Oh really?" He snapped his fingers over his shoulder. A maid appeared from the next room, as if waiting for his signal. She already had a kerchief tied around her neck from where he had fed on her previously. He gestured with his chin at the window, and she gamely went over and began to unbolt the latches.

"I can compel Bridget and her entire stupid entourage in there to go jump off a balcony," Damon growled.

"I don't believe you," I said as calmly as I could. Only Lexi seemed able to control more than one person at once. And Damon wasn't nearly as old as she.

"Or I can stalk them one by one and rip their throats out," he offered instead. "It makes no difference to me."

The maid stepped up onto the sill and began to climb onto the rail.

"*Bastard*," I murmured, rushing over to grab the poor girl before she killed herself. "*Get out of here*," I growled at her, unsure if I was compelling her or not. Suddenly she looked confused and scared, the spell broken. She bolted out of the room, sniffling.

"Why?" I demanded when she had gone. "Why do you

want to marry Lydia? Why is it so important that I marry her sister?"

"If I have to live forever, I might as well do it in style," Damon said, shrugging. "I'm sick of living from person to person, meal to meal, having no place to call home. When I marry Lydia, I'll be rich. A houseful of servants to attend to my every whim . . . to feed my every need," he leered. I wasn't sure he was just talking about blood. "Or, I could just take the money and run. Either way, I'll be a lot better off than I am now. Winfield is *swimming* in money."

"Why involve me?" I asked, feeling weary. "Why not just go off and do whatever it is you need to do, ruining people's lives?"

"Let's just say I have my reasons." Damon flashed me a harlequin's grin.

I shook my head in exasperation. Just past the door of the study, a couple walked arm in arm through the library, in search of a quiet place to talk. Beyond them were the happy noises of the dancing throng, laughing conversations, the tap of heels on the floor. I watched distractedly, picking out Winfield's booming voice as he lectured someone on the basic tenets of capitalism.

"What will you do with them?" I asked. With Damon as son-in-law, Winfield Sutherland's life expectancy had just been drastically reduced—and Lydia's as well.

"Once I have their money? *Pfff.* I don't know," Damon said, throwing his hand up in the air. "I hear San Francisco is fairly exciting—or maybe I'll just go and take that grand tour in Europe you'd always dreamed of."

"Damon—" I began.

"Or I could just live here, like the king I do so want to be," he continued, cutting me off. "Enjoying myself . . ."

I had a horrible image of Damon satisfying his every carnal desire in the Sutherland household.

"I won't let you do this," I said urgently.

"Why do you care?" Damon asked. "I mean, it wasn't *me* tearing through New Orleans. . . . What was your body count toward the end there, brother?"

"I've changed," I pointed out, looking him in the eye.

"Yes, of course," he said. "Just like that. Whatever could have . . . *oh*!" He grinned. "It's Lydia, isn't it? Once again following in my footsteps, brother. Everything I have you just *want*. Like Katherine."

"*I never loved Katherine.* Not the way you did."

I was attracted to her, of course—who wouldn't have been? She was beautiful, charming, and a terrible flirt. Damon hadn't minded her dark side, and in fact seemed to appreciate it. But when I was with her under her heady spell, I just wanted to ignore her vampire side. And when the vervain cleared my thoughts I was repelled by what she was. All of my feelings, deep feelings, for her, had been the stuff of glamour. For Damon, it was all real.

"And I don't love Lydia," I said. "But that doesn't mean I want to see her—or anyone—hurt."

"Then you do exactly as I say, brother, and everyone will be fine. But if you step out of line, even once . . ." Damon dragged a finger across his throat. "Then their blood will be on your hands."

For a long moment, all was silent as Damon and I glared at each other. I had vowed to never harm a human again, to never allow a human to come to harm because of me. I was trapped as neatly and as permanently as if I were still a sideshow vampire at a circus, tied with vervain ropes—and Damon knew it.

I heaved a sigh. "What do you want me to do?"

9

Fifteen minutes later I stood next to my brother at the outskirts of the dance, waiting for the music to stop. Everyone twirled around, their skirts swishing in perfect synchronicity to the music, all of them oblivious to the fact that two dangerous murderers stood among them.

"Follow my lead," Damon said out the side of his mouth.

"Go to hell," I said out the corner of mine, smiling at Margaret as she passed.

"Been there. Not to my liking," he answered, taking two glasses of champagne off a tray and handing one to me.

"*There* you are," Bridget squealed, running up to me.

She bounced up and down with excitement, causing all of the flounces on her dress to rise and fall like a giant stinging jellyfish. She grabbed my arm. "What were you talking about all this time? *Me?*"

I turned and looked at her. She was beautiful and completely off-putting—self-centered, immature, always vying for attention. But Bridget Sutherland didn't deserve to die. I had been responsible for enough deaths in my short time as a vampire. I could never put to right the wrongs I'd committed in those early days, but saving this family from Damon's vengeance was my responsibility. I would not have their blood on my conscience.

"Yes. Yes I was," I answered, and then I drained my drink and motioned for the waiter to bring me another.

"Attention please," Damon called out, tapping on his glass with a silver spoon. The master of the dance, Reginald Chester, squinted at Damon curiously. The orchestra, looking confused, put down their instruments. Mrs. Chester first seemed put out that someone else was taking charge of the dance—but when she saw who it was, she began to beam like Damon was her own son.

The murmuring crowd turned to us: young, old, with feathers, with gems, in wide lace shawls and massive silk dresses, like a flock of tropical birds at a zoo awaiting the keeper who would scatter grain for their supper.

They whispered to one another and nodded, trying to claim connection to him:

"*I had dinner with him last week.*"

"*He was having drinks with the Knoxes, that's where I met him.*"

"*I recommended my best tailor to him.*"

It was difficult to tell if the crowd had been charmed by Damon's natural charisma, or if there was powerful compelling at work. But I wondered again how a vampire as young as Damon could command such Power.

"My new friend and I have an announcement to make," Damon called out, assuming his fake Italian accent once more. Lydia quietly slipped to the front of the crowd, coming to stand near Damon.

"Many of you know the story of the night Miss Sutherland and I first met . . . I, a stranger to your shores, and she, a beautiful damsel in distress . . ."

The crowd smiled adoringly. Hilda and one of her girlfriends exchanged envious looks.

"And in a shocking coincidence, my friend here, Stefan Salvatore, rescued her sister, the equally beautiful and charming Bridget Sutherland, just last night. I can't speak for him," he said, drawing close to Lydia, his glass still raised, his attention still on the crowd, "but for me, it was love at first sight. I've already spoken to her father, and so before anyone else can grab her away from me, I, Count Damon DeSangue, beg Lydia for the honor of her hand in marriage, though I have nothing to offer her beyond my good name and lifelong devotion."

He got down on one knee and whispered, "Lydia?"

Lydia's face flushed prettily. She was taken off guard. Though she was not the sort of girl who really looked forward to being asked to wed in front of a large crowd, she beamed.

"Of course, Damon, with all my heart!" she exclaimed, throwing her arms around him.

The Sutherland family stood together at the front of the crowd. The look on Margaret's face wasn't so much a scowl as disgusted shock and sheer confusion. I knew how she felt, but wondered at her response. Wasn't she under Damon's compulsion to accept him—and me— completely?

Bridget's reaction was equally human, and far more horrible. Her eyes burned with pure, searing jealousy. Maybe there was a tiny bit of relief that her older sister was getting married, which meant that now in turn *she* could. But it was obvious that the youngest Sutherland had been dreaming her whole life of exactly how her perfect suitor would propose, and that it involved being done in public, in front of all her friends and an admiring audience.

The admiring crowd clapped and then Damon's eyes flicked back toward me. Just once. Like he had the power to compel me. And in a manner of speaking, he did. I knew exactly what he wanted me to do.

I drained my second champagne before stepping forward, turning toward Bridget.

Here I went again. It seemed only yesterday that I was in Mystic Falls, yearning to go to school in Charlottesville, waiting out the war in the lazy, endless summer, and being forced to court Rosalyn. Each time I called upon her it was with a leaden ball in my stomach, and each visit was an exercise in frustration and despair. I never wanted to marry her—our parents wished us to marry. My *father* expected us to marry. And so I was forced into an engagement I didn't want, anticipating a marriage I didn't desire.

Once again I was being being forced into a marriage. But perhaps this was all part of the punishment I deserved. And if it meant saving lives . . .

"Bridget." I turned to her, bent at my waist and holding my drink out, toasting her. I was the very form of romantic etiquette, exuding Southern charm the like of which these Yankees rarely saw. "From the very moment I . . ." *Saw your near-lifeless body covered in blood in Central Park and almost finished you off.* ". . . had the fortune to come to you in the hour of your direst need, I just knew you had to be mine. And thanks to the generosity of your parents, I already feel like family. Bridget, will you make this the happiest night of my life?"

With a porcine squeal Bridget threw her arms around me—after first carefully handing her glass of punch to Hilda.

"Good show," Bram clapped, his cheeks flushing even redder. "I knew you were a decent chap! I could tell right away!"

The crowd exploded with cheers and thunderous applause; buckets of champagne were ordered all around. Winfield Sutherland looked so puffed up with pride and joy I feared he would explode. Mrs. Sutherland looked quietly pleased now that the last of her daughters were matched. Only Margaret shook her head angrily before freezing her face into a good show of sisterly pride.

The leader of the dance had a Nebuchadnezzar of champagne brought forth, a giant glass bottle that held the equivalent of twenty bottles' worth of champagne. In an elegant display of sabrage, he took a sword from his butler and dramatically sliced along the bottle, causing the neck to fly off in a beautiful explosion of sparkling golden liquid.

"Let's have the weddings this weekend!" Damon cried

out, as if caught up in the general excitement. "We've waited our whole lives to find these ladies—why wait now?"

Yes, why wait? I thought. Let Damon's games begin.

10

November 6, 1864

Damon is back, though it seems he was never actually gone. He has been watching me, baiting me, controlling me. He is the puppet master and I am his hapless marionette, forced to do his bidding.

Until I saw Damon, I had not realized just how fond I had become of the Sutherlands, of how they eased my loneliness and gave me hope that I might not have to live in exile. Though I knew I had to leave them, I had dared to hope that by proving I could stay in control around them, my journey through this world might ultimately be less solitary.

But Damon knows me all too well. He might
have compelled the Sutherlands to accept me, but
he didn't compel me to stay in their presence. I
could have slipped out this morning, could have
run off in the park, could have disappeared into
the crowd at the ball. And yet I stayed, because,
as Damon no doubt predicted, I liked being part
of a family again, even if just for a few fleeting
days.

Damon's plan terrifies me—precisely because
I don't understand it. Why New York? Why the
Sutherlands? Why involve me? If Damon was
able to orchestrate everything, to so seamlessly
weave his way into the Sutherlands' lives and
pave the way for my arrival, why stage such a
spectacle? Why bother with a marriage? Why not
just take Winfield to the bank and compel him
and the teller to empty his vast accounts? Does
he intend to live as a human? Does he need the
marriage for legitimacy in New York society? Is
he simply intent upon torturing me?

Or is there something I'm missing? Some secret
aim I can't possibly begin to imagine . . .

All I have are questions. And I fear that the
answers won't come until the first dead body
shows up.

Later that Monday afternoon, I stood on the roof deck of one of the most amazing Federal-style houses ever built. Slim columns supported a soaring porch over a formal entrance, to which a grand, curved driveway rolled up as royally as a red carpet. From casement to cornice every detail was thoughtfully considered and never overdone. The dining room, large and oval, was (as near as I could tell) exactly the same as the one in the White House. *The* White House. In our new capital. That's the sort of place the Commandant's House was, as befitted the man who looked after the Brooklyn Naval Yards.

What it lacked in size and modern touches (such as the Sutherlands' residence), it more than made up for in perfectly manicured lawns, a fine orchard, and a spectacular view of Manhattan. The property was perched almost on a cliff surveying the East River and the city that was under the Navy's protection. Commodore Matthew Perry himself had lived there earlier. I sighed at its magnificence.

"No," Bridget said, shaking her head decisively and heading back downstairs, picking up the train of her skirts in a very businesslike way.

Her little entourage followed, laughing good-naturedly.

"It's too white," joked Bram.

"It's too small," added Hilda.

"But it's incredible! The views! The size! The . . ." I said. "What's wrong with this one?"

"*Placement*. It's in Brooklyn," Bridget said, barely acknowledging her fiancé. "No one goes to Brooklyn to be married."

Winfield and his wife looked at each other with old love, clearly remembering their own wedding. Apparently it had been quite modest—he had not made his fortune yet. Neither one of them had minded. And yet they were willing to indulge their youngest daughter in her most expensive flights of fancy.

Lydia smiled and murmured something to Damon, who wasn't really paying attention. She didn't mind where she was married. While it was to be a double feature with us two "happy" couples tying the knot at the same time, she had graciously allowed her sister to decide all the details.

The Sutherlands were at least nominally Episcopal, but apparently neither Damon's nor my religion, or lack thereof, was a bother, nor was a proper church necessary to the proceedings; a family chapel—a very rich family's chapel—would be enough. Bridget was very modern that way.

"So why did we bother seeing those mansions on Prospect Park?" Margaret muttered. "If Brooklyn is out, I mean."

"I rather liked the one with all the Romanesque arches," I said, eager to get this portion of the sham weddings out of the way.

"Fear not, brother," Damon said, chucking me on the shoulder. "Only four more to go. Back in Manhattan."

We clattered down the steep, wooden, and rather old-fashioned stairs to the ground floor, thanking the butler for letting us in. Then it was a walk back down to the Fulton Ferry landing, where a boat would take us across to a veritable caravan of carriages for the long uptown commute.

"This would be a nice place for an ice cream parlor," Lydia remarked, walking around the dock pensively.

"You want an ice cream?" Damon asked, as if to a four-year-old.

If being with Bridget was bad enough, with me constantly cringing at the things that came out of her mouth, the nervous tension of waiting for Damon to say or do something horrible was even worse. I was on pins and needles the entire day. Because Damon *would* say something horrible, at some point, to Lydia, as soon as he tired of playing the game of attentive suitor. His attention span for games—other than ones he was betting on—was incredibly limited.

"Yes," Lydia said. "And there's no ice cream here. And there should be."

"Won't matter," Bridget said, trying to add something

useful to the conversation. "Soon there's going to be a giant bridge and this will all be shaded off and there won't be anything except for loud carriages and the stink of horses."

Bram, the original source of this information, shook his head. "No, Bridgey, the angle is fine. Look where the sun is . . ."

I leaned on a dock railing, surveying our little party. The girls in this setting looked like a scene from a painting, the four ladies' cheeks rosy with sunlight and the exertion of the day, the long ribbons from their straw hats blowing in the wind, their fluffy walking skirts swept up against their legs by the sea breeze. They were all beautiful, and for just a moment I could forget my present situation.

Margaret bought a paper from a newsboy to read on the trip over. It was a fine day for a boat ride and strangely the East River didn't repel me the way fresh running water usually did. Bridget went to sit down inside the ferry, not wanting any more sun on her skin, which was ironic and hilarious considering my own situation. I was relaxing for the first time that day, my face up to the sun, letting my Mediterranean skin take on a bronzed, healthy glow.

And then Margaret plopped down in the seat next to me.

"You seem to be at least a bit more reasonable than the *other* fiancé," Margaret snapped. "Tell me. What do you want with my family. Money? The business? What?"

I groaned inwardly. "You have to believe me," I said, fixing her blue eyes with my own hazel ones. Without compelling her, I willed my voice to sound as genuine as I could. I took her arms in my hands, which was bold, but I needed her to understand. "I am not after Bridget's wealth. All I want is your family's safety and happiness. I swear to you by whatever you want."

"That's just the problem. I don't know what your word is worth. I don't know you. *Nobody* knows you," Margaret said. Sighing, she took off her hat. "It's just . . . so . . . odd. I can see why Bridget likes you, you're certainly handsome and well-mannered. . . ."

I cast my eyes down, embarrassed.

"But really—no papers, no history, just an escapee of the South? This is *Bridget* we're talking about. She wanted Papa to take us all on a tour of Europe so she could capture the heart of a king, or prince, or at least a duke. Nothing less than royalty for her. And no offense, you're about as far from royalty as one can get."

"Well, and Lydia got her count, I suppose."

"Yes," Margaret said thoughtfully. She eyed me, pushing a black tendril of hair back behind her ear. "And what about Damon DeSangue . . ."

I shrugged, trying to look innocent.

"What do you think of him? The two of you have been . . . unusually close since your double declarations of love."

I stared into the distance south, where the mighty Hudson and East rivers joined and became the sea. I shaded the city from my eyes, blocking it out, and the sun was bright white and rose over ancient, exotic waters.

How much could I tell her without endangering her? She seemed to be the only one in the family with a sensible head on her shoulders. I thought once more about Katherine and whether my family would have been better prepared with some warning.

"Don't trust him," I finally admitted, hoping I wasn't putting her at greater risk. "I don't."

"Hm." She looked over at Damon, who was talking animatedly with Bram and Winfield. "Neither do I."

Bridget had chosen the next few venues to visit as far away as it was possible to get from where we were. The mansion of the Richards was near Fort Tryon on the northern tip of Manhattan, while the Fulton Ferry dock was at the southeastern end.

The slow ride in our carriages from downtown gave me an almost panopticon's view of city life. Slowly going up Fifth

Avenue, I was amazed by the sheer difference in fortune of the people who made their home in New York—from the often shoeless newsboys and *schmatta*, or rag-sellers, to people like Winfield, who sat in his gilded private carriage, puffing on a cigar.

We stopped for lunch about halfway there at the Mount Vernon Hotel on Sixty-first Street, where Bridget continued to discuss her outfit for the wedding.

". . . and Darla had her dress in muslin, out of respect for the war, but it's almost over, and I think I should have a new pair of earrings, don't you, Papa? Stefan, darling, there is the most fantastic pair of pearl earrings . . ."

Damon cleared his throat. "Bridget, you should absolutely have new earrings. And your outfit sounds good enough to eat, don't you agree, Stefan?"

I stood up from the table, unable to enjoy the nice repast of cold chicken, fresh bread, fish, and tea that had been set before us, and unable to listen to another word of my fiancée's mindless prattling or my brother's endless teasing.

"I must go take some air," I excused myself, and would have stumbled over the bench on my speedy way out if I didn't have the grace of a vampire. I should not have been exhausted; I'd endured far worse. Living hungry in the middle of Central Park and hunting small prey was far more physically demanding than sitting in a carriage, looking at houses, and listening to the youngest member of the Sutherland family babble on about meaningless things. But as I had not fed since the squirrel the day before, I was famished and weak, as if I was enduring a transatlantic journey.

A quick, silent trip to the kitchens revealed exactly what I had hoped—rats, of course. Not too many, and mostly in the breezeway between the cold house and the pantry. With a flash of my hand I grabbed one and broke its neck, sucking the poor thing dry, all without losing control. It was easy, with such disgusting fare.

A low noise, a muffled sigh, made me turn and look up guiltily, rat blood leaking down my lips.

Damon stood there holding a waitress around her throat, fangs out and ready to feast. She had the dumb, slightly breathless look of someone who was under a spell.

"I see we both slipped out for the same thing," Damon said, pleased. He raised a lip in disgust at the rat in my hand. "Although, really, you can do better."

He lifted his head back, ready to tear—

"Please—don't . . ." I put up my hand helplessly. "Please don't kill her," I begged.

Damon paused. "All right," he said gamely. "I won't *kill* her. As an early wedding present! Just for you."

I closed my eyes, seeing the horror of the future before me. By implying he wasn't going to kill *this* girl, as a present, there was the assumption that there would of course be other murders, later on.

The following morning, I clutched the soft linen sheets up to my neck, as I had when I was a child. With my eyes squeezed shut, I could almost pretend I was home again. That Damon and I were still human and having our usual brotherly quarrels. That our father was somewhere on the plantation, working. That Katherine was alive.

No—wait. *That we had never met Katherine.*

Or . . . maybe I was in bed at Lexi's house, unsure about my new life, but accepted in this new home of fellow vampires.

I slowly came fully awake, and my fantasies crumbled against reality. I was in the Sutherlands' house, still a captive of their generosity and my brother's threats, an uneager groom being run quickly into an unwanted wedding.

The Sutherlands weren't terribly formal but nevertheless expected everyone to show up at breakfast. My dressing went perhaps slower than it might have normally, as I adjusted my sock garters until they were perfect, fiddled with my cuffs, and ran my hands through my hair. I didn't much like looking in mirrors in those days. I hated who I saw there.

By the time I finally made it downstairs to breakfast, the entire family was well into their meal. Mrs. Sutherland greeted me with a warm maternal smile that tore at my insides. Though I felt genuinely fond toward her, she was *compelled* to accept me.

"Good morning," I mumbled, slinking into my place. "Is there any coffee?"

"You seem a bit down today, m'boy," Winfield said, tucking his watch into his breast pocket. "And a bit thin, may I add. You definitely need fattening up before the wedding—I think I'll take you to the club today. They do a wonderful lamb and pudding."

Lydia gave me an apologetic smile. With a shock I realized that a pretty rose-pink scarf encircled her neck, neatly covering the usual spot for a vampire bite.

Damon had fed on her.

I turned my head from the coffee that had been placed before me, my stomach churning. Unconsciously, I touched my neck where Katherine used to bite me, remembering the pain and pleasure all wound up together so sickly. Was it a message to me? To remind me of what would happen if I failed to marry Bridget?

"Stefan! Don't go to the club until later! We have a full day today," Bridget warned. "We absolutely must, must, *must* go visit Bram's family. They just *love* Damon—Brammy's been taking him to all of the latest places, like that bar that serves real English-style Pimm's Cups! I'll have to wear my new blue muslin. To their house, not to the bar, naturally. It isn't a suitable place for ladies. Fanny wanted blue muslin for her trousseau, but her engagement didn't work out, poor thing. . . ."

The door to the kitchen opened, and Damon stepped through. "Good morning, all," he crowed, bright-eyed and chipper. He looked rested and sated as he gave Lydia a flirty bow and me a nasty wink.

My shoulders clenched. "What are you doing here, Damon?" I asked in as innocent a tone as I could muster.

"You didn't hear?" He sat down at the table and unfolded his napkin with a flourish. "Winfield begged me to move in."

"Oh." I pushed my chair back from the table, plastering a wobbly smile on my face to mask my anger. "Er, Damon, would you mind joining me in the foyer for a moment?"

Damon grinned at me. "But I just sat down and I'm ever so hungry."

"It will take but a minute," I said through clenched teeth.

Lydia looked at me curiously, but after a beat, Damon scraped his chair back and followed me to the foyer. "Milady, I'll return shortly."

The second we were out of earshot, I turned to my brother. "You are *unbelievable*. You're moving in now?"

"Why thank you," Damon said with a facetious bow. "And yes. Were you not listening last night when I talked about all the amazing . . . *amenities* the Sutherland abode has to offer?"

The room began to spin around me as rage overtook me. My patience with Damon's game was over.

"Why bother with all of . . . this?" I demanded. "These shenanigans? If you're so powerful, why not just go into a bank and *make* them give you all of the gold in their vaults?"

"I suppose I could, but where's the fun in that?"

"The fun?" I echoed in disbelief. "You're doing this for *fun*?"

Damon's eyes hardened. "Tracks, brother. You're not thinking ahead." He frowned and brushed some imaginary lint off my jacket. "Yes, I could just steal the money and leave town. But we're going to be around *forever*. Or at least I am. And compulsion doesn't always take. In case you didn't notice, Margaret remains quite stubborn, and having her or Winfield, should he ever shake my Power, go around waving my picture and calling me a thief . . . well, I can't have that. It's much easier—and more fun—just to inherit it."

I gazed at the door that separated us from the happily dining Sutherlands. "Inherit it? As in, upon death?"

"What? Why, brother, what exactly are you implying?" he asked, pretending to be hurt. "You keep your half of the bargain, and I don't go on a killing spree. Remember? I gave you my word."

"No, Damon," I said. "You said if I didn't marry Bridget you would start killing everyone in that room. You specifically did *not* say anything about what would happen *after* we were married."

"Good point," Damon said, nodding. "I'd like to kill a few people in their circle. Starting with that sycophant Bram. I think he has a thing for my Lydia, you know," he added with mock anger.

"Damon," I growled.

His eyes narrowed. "You take care of your wife. I'll take care of mine."

I looked at my brother sharply. "So then you do plan to kill Winfield after he signs over his fortune?"

"For that, you will just have to stick around and see."

"I won't let you hurt any of them," I promised through a clenched jaw.

"You can't stop me. *Whatever* I choose to do," Damon hissed back.

We glared at each other. My hands curled into fists. He shifted his stance, ready for a fight.

At that moment Mrs. Sutherland poked her head into the foyer. "Boys? Everything okay out here?"

"Yes, ma'am," Damon answered graciously. "We were just acquainting ourselves." He pointed the door to the kitchen and gave a slight bow. "After you, Stefan."

Reluctantly, I passed back into the kitchen, Damon close on my heels.

"So tomorrow we pick out our suits," Damon said. He was acting as though we were continuing a mundane discussion from the foyer, rather than just having ended an argument over the fates of everyone in the room. "Stefan, we should match! Why, Bridget, weren't you just saying last night how someone, I forget who, matched her sister at another wedding? Silk or something?"

He knew. He was my brother and he knew precisely how to torment me. Eternally.

"Yes, of course, Damon," Bridget said with a gratified smile, turning to me. "*Stefan*, you have to hear this. I thought about matching me and Lydia, but I'm not sure the effect would be as dramatic, what with Lydia's figure . . ."

I slowly sank down at the table, drowning in her words—and the knowledge that Damon was right. I had never been able to stop my brother, especially not when it mattered most.

12

The next few days drifted by, chock-full of wedding planning and menu sampling. At night, the Sutherlands settled into a steady routine. Mrs. Sutherland took to the sewing room, teaching Lydia to make quilts and bonnets. Bridget indulged in a late-night beauty regime that involved brushing her hair in one hundred strokes and lathering herself in cream that I could smell all the way from the parlor. Winfield always retired to his study with a tumbler of brandy, perusing the paper or going over his accounting books.

I'd taken to pacing the first floor, coming up with plans to ferry the Sutherlands to safety only to shoot down most of my ideas. I also now needed to plan my feedings. My steady diet of city animals was harder to keep up now that I was under the watchful eye of every Sutherland

and servant. It was almost like they *expected* me to try and make a break for it, though it was impossible to know how much of that was genuine wariness versus Damon compelling them to follow me. Sometimes I managed to slip away, whether up to the roof or silently down to the backyard to try and find a rat or pigeon or even a mouse to satisfy my needs. Hazel, the house cat, was off limits of course, but fortunately her wild tomcat friends were not.

Damon had no such nutritional problems. Nor did he care much about secrecy. He came and went as he pleased, doing God knows what in the darkest corners of the city. I often saw a maid or manservant summoned to his suite in the coldest hours of the night as I skulked about tending to my own needs. For my brother, life with the Sutherlands was like living in a grand hotel—he attended dinners in his honor and was feted all around town at the top establishments. He was a prince and New York was his adoring kingdom.

When Damon arrived home on Thursday, Winfield poked his head out of the study.

"Oh, good. I'm glad you're here," Winfield said, holding out two glasses of whiskey. "Please come join me."

There was a stray drop of blood carelessly smeared on the corner of Damon's mouth. Anyone else would have assumed it was a shaving cut. Suddenly the cozy study seemed suffocating and the corners darker.

Damon casually wiped his lips, his eyes on me, then threw himself down on the couch next to his future father-in-law, less like an Italian count and more like . . . well, Damon. "Good evening, sir." The fact that he dropped his fake accent in their presence highlighted just how under his thrall this family was.

"I wanted to have a chat with the two of you about your futures," Winfield began, chomping on his cigar.

"Oh, I have big plans, I'm thinking long-term," Damon said. "Living here with the family, of course. I love close kin."

My throat went dry and I ran a hand through my hair, beginning to panic, reminded once again that I had no idea what Damon really wanted.

"I think I should like to go into business for myself," Damon began to say. But then the door of the study slammed open and Margaret came striding in.

"Papa!"

Without a word to either of us she threw a copy of the day's *Post* down into her father's hands and tapped at an article. "Read this."

Winfield fished around in his pockets for his glasses and slid them on, peering at the paper.

"Sutherland house is scandalized as two penniless suitors sweep away the last of the eligible Sutherland girls. Heartbroken sons of bankers, politicians, and empires of capital complain

bitterly about the sudden move. Is it blackmail, some wonder?
An unnamed source close to the family claims that . . . Oh, rub-
bish," he said, throwing the paper aside and taking off his
glasses. "People talk about the silliest things."

"We will be *ruined*," Margaret said, almost pleading.
She completely ignored Damon's and my presence. "At the
very least, can't you see how it would be bad for business?"

"Don't you think you should leave that sort of talk
for the menfolk?" Damon asked lazily, returning to his
accented English. But his ice-blue eyes bored straight
into her head, as if he wished he could put a bullet there.
I stood up, placing myself between Margaret and him.
She didn't seem to notice his hatred, or the danger she
was in.

"I understand your concerns," I said quickly. I had to
convince her to drop this, for her own sake. "But believe
me, I want nothing but the best for your family."

"And in fact, we menfolk were just talking about business," Winfield added. "Damon, you were saying?"

"All I need is a small sum of cash," my brother said, turning his head and effectively cutting Margaret out of the
conversation. "Which will allow me to travel to my home
country and start picking out vendors for exports. . . ."

Margaret let out a gasp. "You're not actually thinking
of giving him *more* than his dowry?"

"Don't be greedy, pet," Winfield said, shushing her

with a patronizing gesture. "It's just seed money to get him on his way. . . ."

"Have you gone *crazy?*" she demanded. "You don't even know this man. Let him work for you first. Or give him one of your smaller businesses to run."

Damon rose from his seat, coldly furious. I tried to take Margaret's arm, but she shook me off. She pulled herself up to her full height, staring straight back into his eyes. Though she wasn't quite as pretty as either of her younger sisters, she was certainly imposing.

"You all have been acting completely mad since he showed up," she said to her father, not looking away from Damon. "Letting him—and *him*"—she gestured at me— "become practically *members* of this family, live under our roof, share our bread, and then offer them cash and your daughters and everything else! Doesn't *anyone* think this is strange besides me?"

Winfield looked upset, but confused.

Damon widened his eyes.

"Stop," he compelled her. "Just accept Stefan and me—we're here to stay."

She looked at him for a long moment. I waited for her eyes to glaze over, for her pupils to dilate ever so slightly. But all she did was shake her head in disgust. "Your phony 'count' act might work with other people, but not me. I want no part of this."

I stared at her, stunned, as she stormed out. I'd never seen Damon fail to compel someone, not even when he'd been young and weak. I inhaled deeply, searching for hints of vervain, anything to explain what had just happened. But there was nothing there.

All I could do was hope that whatever it was, it would continue to keep Margaret safe.

13

That night I lay in bed, gazing up at the ceiling. The moon shone through the gauzy white curtains, and the house hummed with activity, a melee of footsteps, heartbeats, and mice skittering inside the walls. It felt as though the entire house were alive, with the exception, of course, of myself and Damon. The Sutherlands had no idea, but when they'd opened their home to me, they had invited Death in. I was a cancer on their happy existence, and soon the darkness would spread, eating through their world until there was nothing left.

Though I was no willing participant in Damon's twisted plan, it would be no different from how Katherine insinuated herself into my life and decimated the entire Salvatore family. Like it or not, this family's well-being rested squarely on my shoulders. If Damon killed them, their blood would be on my hands, too. But how could I stop him? I was so much weaker than my brother, and I had no plans to begin feeding on humans again for fear that I'd be unable to stop.

I rose from bed and pushed the curtains aside with a violent flick. As I stared at the moon, that orb that had witnessed so much of my ill-doing, I replayed the conversation we'd had with Margaret over and over in my head. The firm set of her jaw. The clear tone of her eyes. The way her lucid blue eyes had sized up me and Damon, as though she could see straight through our skin to our unbeating hearts. Winfield was ready to sign his fortune over to Damon, yet his daughter remained immune to my brother's Power.

But how?

The only protection I knew against vampires was vervain, but I'd not inhaled its cloying scent since arriving in New York. When trying to draw out Katherine, my father had spiked my whiskey with vervain, sending Katherine into a miasmic fit when she drank my blood. If only my father had thought to protect me sooner, he and I might still be in Mystic Falls, poring over accounting books as I studied to take over Veritas.

Sliding the window open, I stepped out onto the narrow balcony. The night was eerily still. No wind rustled the trees, and even the pigeons that roosted on the neighbor's roof were quiet. My balcony faced east, toward the muddy East River and the narrow spit of land they called Blackwell's Island, where the city had recently rebuilt the lunatic asylum. A wry smile twisted my lips. If only I could check Damon in there.

But then I let out a groan and clutched the wrought-iron rail with my hands. I had to stop wishing and hoping and thinking of millions of *if only*s. I could not wish Damon into oblivion and I could not rewrite the past. What was done was done. Even at my peak Power, I could not cause the world to spin backward, could not turn back time and undo what Katherine did to me and my family. But I was not powerless over the future. I had free will, I had experience, and I had the choice to fight.

Hoisting myself up on the rail, I leaped to the roof, landing on the tar with a soft thud. New York was a large city, and someone, somewhere, had to grow vervain or at least have dried sprigs. I'd run up and down the streets until I caught the telltale scent of the herb. Spiking Lydia's drinks would be impossible—Damon was feeding from her—but if I could just sprinkle some in Winfield's whiskey . . .

I ran across the roof, preparing to jump to that of the neighbor, before scaling down their fire escape to the street below.

"Where are you going, brother?" The cheery words sliced through the night like gunshot, and I froze on the ledge.

Slowly, I turned around to face a smiling Damon. He looked ready for the second part of his evening jaunt, wearing a three-piece suit and twirling a gold cane in his hand. I recognized it immediately—it had belonged to Callie's father, the man who had imprisoned Damon, torturing him and starving him before forcing him to do battle with a mountain lion. Damon must have stolen it after he killed Callie.

Unbidden, an image of Callie bloomed in my mind. Her kind green eyes smiling at me, the freckles that dusted every inch of her body, the way she had so bravely given herself to me on the shore of the lake, offering her blood even though she knew what I was and what I could do to her. . . .

Her dead, twisted body lying in the grass behind Lexi's house.

"You bastard," I said in a low, fury-filled voice that I barely recognized as my own. Rage that had been building for weeks with no outlet tore through my veins, and I felt as though my muscles were on fire. With a growl, I threw myself at him. "Why won't you just let me be?"

Our bodies collided, like stone on stone. Startled, Damon fell backward, but instantly he pushed me off and flipped to his feet. He wrapped his arms around my neck with a vise-like grip. "If you were so desperate to be free of me, you shouldn't have forced me to become a vampire with you," he hissed, all traces of joviality gone from his demeanor. I struggled to free myself, but his knee pressed more forcefully into my spine, pinning me to the roof. "You were the one who urged me to become what I am—to see what Katherine gave us as a gift rather than a curse."

"Trust me," I gasped, trying to twist from his grip. "I would take it back if I could."

"*Tsk-tsk*," Damon chided. "Didn't Father teach you that part of being a man is living with your choices?" He pressed my cheek into the tar roof, scraping open the skin there. "Then again, you were such a disappointment to him at the end—not wanting to marry Rosalyn, taking up with a vampire, killing him . . ."

"You were *always* a disappointment," I spat. "I should have killed you when I had the chance."

Damon let out a dry laugh. "Well, that would have been a shame, because then I couldn't do this."

The pressure on my spine abated as Damon hoisted me up by the back of the shirt.

"What are you—" I started.

Before I could finish, Damon launched me forward with the force of a lit cannon. My body careened through the night air, and for a brief, weightless moment, I wondered if

I was flying. Then the hard pavement of the alley between the Sutherlands' and their neighbor's home rushed up to greet me, and my bones cracked loudly on the impact.

I groaned, pain radiating through my limbs as I rolled to my back, blood dripping down my face. I lay like that for hours, staring at the stars until my Power healed me, resetting my bones and stitching up the gash in my cheek more swiftly than the most skilled medic could.

But when I stood, a new pain shot through my chest. Because there on the brick wall of the Sutherlands' home, written in red ink that could only be blood, were three terrifying words:

I'm always watching.

14

On Friday Winfield took Damon and me to get fitted for a custom suit. A visit to Pinotto's Tailoring might have been fun at some other point in my life—as it had been the night I went shopping with Lexi in New Orleans. Pasquale Pinotto was a master of his craft, descended from a long line of tailors to kings and queens of Europe. With his pince-nez glasses and chalk and measuring tape around his neck, he could have been someone out of a fairy tale. I enjoyed trying to speak the few words of Italian I knew to him; he took pleasure in it as well, though he corrected my accent. Damon, of course, pretended that he only wanted to speak English now that he was in America—which is how he got around the tailor's delight at meeting a fellow countryman.

"Look at this." Damon held up a bolt of scarlet red silk to his face. "We could have our jackets lined with it. Doesn't it just bring out the color in my lips? Or . . . Lydia's neck?" He moved it to the side, just about where the fang wounds would have been on him.

Winfield looked confused. "She has taken to wearing scarves around her neck, lately. Is that what you mean? It's dashed peculiar—she never used to."

Damon flicked him a quick look, a flash of surprise and annoyance so fast only I caught it. It was interesting that Mr. Sutherland noticed the subtle changes occurring around him, even if he was ultimately powerless against Damon's compulsion. Although any safety the rich old man had was in staying completely ignorant of my brother's schemes.

I leaned against the wall for support, tension exhausting me. I felt claustrophobic among all the rolls of expensive fabric and labyrinthine rooms of mirrors and sewing machines, as trapped in that room as I was in my life.

Mr. Sutherland made his way to a chair to rest his ponderous bulk. He seemed a touch fidgety—he kept reaching for his cigar, but he was not allowed to smoke one of his famous cigars in the atelier, as the smoke would ruin the fabric.

"Now here is some cloth I am thinking you will like," Signor Pinotto said, presenting us with black wool crepe so fine and soft it might have been silk. "I get it from a tiny village in Switzerland. They work . . ."

"Leave the cloth to me," Winfield said, twirling an unlit cigar in his hand. "*I* know the business. Let the young men pick out whatever style they want."

Damon started looking through the jackets, pulling one out and holding it against him to see how it fit.

"In this morning coat and that black crepe, we'll look like real creatures of the night," Damon observed. "Don't you think so, Stefan?"

"Yes, yes we will," I agreed stonily.

"Here, try this on." Damon tossed me a smaller version of the jacket. Dutifully, I took off my own and put it on. The jacket fit me well except for being too big in the shoulders and chest. Damon was distracted by the tailor and Winfield, discussing patterns and linings and buttons. It occurred to me in that moment that I could leap out the window and run away. Would my brother actually carry through on all of his threats? Would he really kill the Sutherlands—or worse?

But then I thought of the message in blood and realized I would never let the world find out the answer to that question. I wanted no more deaths on my conscience.

"Is that the sort of thing young men prance around town in these days?" Winfield asked, frowning at my jacket. "I've never really been a—what did you call it?—'creature of the night.'"

Damon gave him a cold smile. "Never say never."

And then Damon was suddenly standing next to me in front of the mirror, buttoning up his jacket and fluffing out the tails. Very assiduously he fixed mine as well.

"Well, would you look at that," he said to our reflections, putting an arm around my shoulders. "We could almost *be brothers*."

"We *were* brothers at one time," I hissed so quietly that only Damon's highly tuned ears could hear. "Though you are now as alien to me as the devil himself."

"Eh?" Winfield looked up. "You do resemble each other a little. The . . . hair. And the . . . face." He waved a hand vaguely at us. Then he smiled widely. "I'll have a whole set of matching grandchildren! Dozens of them, dandling on my knees."

Damon grinned. "Absolutely. I plan on having a large family, Mr. Sutherland. It's important that my *bloodline* goes on."

"*You're really pushing it*," I said.

"*I haven't even started*," he whispered, smiling.

"*Oh really? Then what was that message you left for me in blood?*" I said.

Damon's forehead crinkled. "*Message?*"

"Actually, I rather like the scarlet." Winfield held a bolt

of the fabric in his hands, and didn't seem to notice the tension in the air. "It's perfect. Damon *DeSangue*—bloodred, or of blood, right?"

Damon looked surprised. I was taken off guard, too.

"I speak four languages, boys," Winfield said with a bit of a growl in his grin. "And can read another four. I-tal-ian is just one."

So Sutherland wasn't quite the buffoon he appeared to be. There were layers in him, and of course there had to be for such a successful businessman.

"And speaking of languages, *ho bisogno di vino*, something to wet my throat. I brought something from my own cellar, a fantastic amontillado. Care to join me?"

"I really could drain a good Sutherland dry just about now," Damon said gamely, clapping me on the shoulder like our future father-in-law did.

I slumped in despair. When we'd first become vampires, I'd wanted nothing more than to spend eternity with my brother. But now I couldn't wait to be rid of him.

The night before the wedding, I stood staring out the window of my bedroom. A beautiful quarter-moon shown through the ornately paned glass. It felt like the entire nighttime world was teasing me, calling out: *Come play. Come hunt. Come disappear into the darkness.* My skin prickled whenever a hint of the night air breezed through, and my nostrils flared at the thousand and one scents it carried.

I am not meant to stay captive inside at night. . . . I had thought I was miserable in the park hunting squirrels, but here I was trapped by my word, by my guilt, by these stupid walls, by a family of humans under a spell, by my brother.

Mrs. Sutherland came in earlier that evening. She didn't say much, just patted my hand and pinched my cheek, telling me not to worry, the wedding would soon be over and then we all—*we all*—could get back to the normal happy business of being a family.

Little did she know that after Damon was through with them, the Sutherlands would never be able to be normal or happy again.

A knock at the door interrupted my thoughts. I turned and tightened the nice silk smoking jacket Winfield had loaned me, wondering if Mrs. Sutherland had left something behind. But then the door cracked open and a pink, mischievous face poked through.

"Bridget," I half-groaned. I looked around me desperately, as if some sort of exit would suddenly appear that I could escape through.

She giggled and suddenly shoved her way in, slamming the door behind her, leaning against it like she had just shut out an invading army.

"*Stefan*," Bridget said in what she probably thought was a sexy, dulcet tone. She was dressed in a chiffon robe with giant chenille cabbage roses. Underneath, instead of a simple nightgown, she wore a complicated corseted dress made of bright pink silk with a rose-red sash that left her shoulders and neck bare.

"Bridget," I said warningly, backing up. My head hit one of the beams of the four-poster bed.

"I thought maybe we could start the honeymoon early," she whispered, pushing herself into my arms.

"Uh—" I stammered.

Her cheeks were red and her eyes were heavy-lidded. Despite Damon's compulsions, she was also under the sway of her own emotions, stirred to amorous feelings for the man she was about to marry.

She pushed me—with remarkably strong arms—down on to the bed and fell upon me, crushing me under wave after wave of silk. Her breasts heaved over the corset, and I could feel her warm skin through my robe.

I had a perfect view of her bare white neck. Her heart pumped quickly, giving her skin a hot, rosy glow and filling my senses with her blood. I could smell it all over her, salty and warm and human. A shiver went through my body as her chest pressed against mine, and I could feel the pain begin along my jaw. Such a sweet pain—and it had been such a long time since I had had human blood. . . .

It couldn't hurt, part of me said. She wouldn't mind me biting her, even without compulsion. It didn't have to be painful, and she might even enjoy it. Before I knew what I was doing I had pressed my lips to her shoulder, just to feel the skin, to take a little lick . . .

She felt me moving beneath her and misinterpreted it, kissing me harder and getting into a more comfortable position, entwining her legs in mine.

"*No!*"

I managed to get control of myself and shoved her off

me. I didn't mean to do it so forcefully, but even in my weakened state I was still several times stronger than a human. She fell to the end of the bed, against one of the posts, looking shocked.

And then she began to cry.

"You . . . don't want me . . ." she wailed, fat droplets of tears rolling down her cheeks.

"Bridget, no, I . . ." My fangs retracted and I was aching with the pain and my need for blood. "It's just . . . we're getting married *tomorrow*, Bridget. Just one more day. If we wait until it's . . . uh . . . proper, it will be even more special. Just think, we'll have completed a . . . beautiful day . . . with you in your beautiful, uh . . ."

"Cream brocade with Flemish lace on the sleeves and bodice and an ivory satin sash with a veil of matching ivory silk flowers," she sniffled.

"Right." I touched her elbow delicately and tilted her chin up so she had to look at me. She wiped the tears off her face with a piece of her robe. "Let my first night with you be with that image of you in my mind, my blushing bride."

She nodded, sniffing again, giving me a faint smile. "All right."

Then she giggled again, back to her old self, and flounced off the bed and to the door.

"Good night . . . *lover*," she cooed before exiting.

As soon as she was gone I fell back on the bed, muffling a groan in my pillow. It did nothing to abate my frustration. I stood, pacing from the window to the door, wanting to leave, to escape, to hunt, to do *something*. But I had no choice, no option. I was trapped in this room, in this situation, in the terrible in-betweenness of being neither a human nor a monster.

I ripped the pillow straight in two, feathers exploding around the room like a white powder keg.

Damn you, Damon, I thought violently, *for putting me in this position. And damn you, too, Katherine, for beginning all this.*

November 12, 1864

Life with Damon is like playing chess with a mad person. I can think of a thousand different possibilities to defend against, a thousand different moves he could make, and then he goes and changes the rules of the game.

It's just his newfound predilection for casual violence that makes him so incalculable, but the way he revels in it. Though blood is our diet, we as vampires at least have a modicum of self-will. Damon doesn't have to let his dark side win, and yet he embraces it.

I view this change in him with horror and

guilt, as I was the one who set him down the path of the vampire. Katherine was the one who changed him, but I force-fed him his first human.

After seeing his message to me I can't consider leaving the Sutherlands until I have figured out a way to keep them all safe. What my brother did to Callie . . . it obviously isn't beyond him to just dispose of the entire family once they serve their purpose.

But when will he take action? At the wedding? After the wedding? After the honeymoon? Next year? Could I spirit the girls away somewhere? Could I convince them to hide? Could I compel them to? Damon managed to find me here, could he find me—or them—anywhere?

I have to come up with a plan, in case Damon doesn't just leave town with his newfound fortune.

Of course, the simplest solution would be to kill Damon.

Voilà—one maniacal, insane, unpredictable, murderous vampire gone, the world, and myself, a thousand times safer. That's assuming I could do it. I am so much weaker than he is, it would have to be done by surprise or guile or something *equally underhanded, like a knife in the back. Like he killed Callie.*

There isn't any point in thinking that way. I will not stoop to his level. He is my brother. And as awful as he is, he is the only relative left to me.

The next day, time flew by as if it had nothing better to do than gallop me toward matrimony. Before I knew it, I'd been stuffed into my suit, force-fed pancakes, and spirited over one hundred blocks north to the altar, where I stood awaiting my fate, as the Sutherlands unknowingly awaited their own.

Damon and I stood side by side in Woodcliff Manor's great hall—the pretty family chapel nearby was far too small for Bridget's tastes. The Richards were kind enough to let her use their home at the tip of Manhattan Island. It was really more of a castle than a home, with gray towers, parapets, and decorative portcullises, all made from the gray rock that jutted seamlessly out of the rocky promontory on which it sat.

Not so far from there, outside the arched gothic windows, were the remains of Fort Tryon, the site of a sad defeat of Continental forces under George Washington by the British.

My thoughts drifted as I imagined redcoats and scrappy American soldiers and puffs of gunpowder . . . and then something occurred to me. *Katherine* could have witnessed such a battle. I never asked how old she was—perhaps Damon did—but she was far older than her appearance suggested. She had probably witnessed events I only read about in history books.

I shivered at the thought, but the chill was instantly dispelled by the incredible heat in the room. Damon and I stood in front of a crowd of more than two hundred of New York's finest socialites, all sitting uncomfortably in hastily pulled together pews. They had no idea how dangerous it was for them to be there.

I pulled at my collar and tie, which suddenly felt too tight, my vision blurring. The room shifted and morphed, and for just a second, the finery and skin of every wedding attendee melted off as though they'd been caught up in a blaze. Skin flaked off like corn husks, leaving behind pure-white bone and twisted tendons.

"Stefan!" Damon hissed, elbowing me. I realized then that I was clutching his arm. "Do I need to call a medic for you?" he asked sarcastically.

I shook my head, wondering what illness had overcome me. The crowd came back into focus, alive, happy, laughing, and fanning themselves discreetly.

Even I had to admit that Mrs. Sutherland had done a fantastic job working with Mrs. Richards and her housekeepers. A rich red carpet had been laid out, and it was

scattered with so many rose petals you could scarcely
see the fabric beneath. Pink, white, and deep, deep red,
it looked like a beautiful trail through a magnificent rose
garden. Garlands of expensive and exotic flowers hung
along the pews, and the scent of orange and lemon was
heavy in the air. Overhead hung giant balls of flowers like
fireworks in petals. Vases in every gothic arched nook and
cranny held elegant arrangements of grasses and blooming
branches of quince, enhancing the woodland effect.

Everyone wore full formal regalia, tailcoats for the men,
some with diplomatic sashes. Heavy moiré silks for the
older women, lighter for the young women, yards and yards
of fabric swirled around their feet like more rose petals.
Hats were decked out in plumes and gems and sometimes
entire birds. And the real heirloom jewelry had been pulled
out for this occasion, pearls and diamonds and rubies on
every neck and wrist, some gems the size of my thumb.

All the women had fans, of course, made from silk and
painted in Japan or England, and they tried to flutter them
delicately, but most wound up just flapping them as fast as
they could. The ladies' countenances remained stubbornly
rosy despite their efforts to keep pale.

Everyone whispered and talked excitedly, and of
course I could tune in to any conversation I felt like listening to with my enhanced hearing. I almost didn't mean to,
because it was the same in every seat:

". . . so quick. Only met a month ago. Did you hear the story? He was so chivalrous. . . ."

". . . lucky girl. I hope my Lucretia marries as well. . . ."

"Apparently, the youngest Beaumont threw herself at DeSangue, but he only had eyes for Lydia. . . ."

". . . such a handsome man! *And* a count! . . ."

". . . yes, but who's that other one again? Marrying Bridget?"

I closed my eyes, wishing I could close my ears. How I longed to be back in my grotto in the park.

"Seems like old times, doesn't it, brother?" Damon sighed, adjusting one of his cuffs. "In another life, you and Rosalyn would be married already."

"Shut up," I said. He was right, though. If Katherine hadn't killed my childhood playmate, I would have married her. Back then, I thought a forced marriage with someone I didn't love was the worst fate imaginable. How innocent I was. . . .

I continued smiling, although it must have looked forced by that point. My eyes darted over the crowd, seeking out anyone in a badly matched scarf. That morning I had managed to grab and drain a pair of white doves, initially intended to be released as a romantic gesture after the wedding ceremony. But when was the last time Damon had fed? Or did he have a big, bloody feast planned?

"Look at us, together," Damon whispered, nodding at someone in the crowd and smiling. "We make quite a handsome pair."

"I'm doing this," I whispered, "to save lives. Now be quiet."

Damon rolled his eyes. "You're no fun, brother. I hope you develop a sense of humor soon, or it's going to be a looooong eternity."

The wedding march began, saving me from having to respond.

Margaret's husband and Bram, ushers, came down the aisle first. The remaining ushers were callow youths who flirted outrageously with the bridesmaids they escorted. The girls wore pretty matching peach gowns and absolutely giant hats . . . but I noticed that one had a slightly different accessory from the rest. Hilda wore a hastily tied kerchief around her neck.

I glared at Damon.

He shrugged. "I got a little peckish waiting around."

In truth, I was a little relieved—it meant he wasn't starving himself in anticipation of something later.

Finally came Winfield, proudly striding down the aisle with a daughter on each arm. Lydia walked regally and easily. She wore a simple white gown of heavy material whose folds rustled with her movements. It went to the top of her neck and the bottom of her wrists, and its only ornamentation was a line of pearl buttons down the front. A net veil hung behind her, floating down her back. She looked like a fairy-tale queen, and smiled with a secretive look that only added to her beauty.

On Winfield's left arm was Bridget, wearing her brocade and satin. She actually looked quite beautiful, if a bit overdone. An enormous lace veil perched on top of her head like a crown. It was hard to imagine, now, that I'd ever seen anything of Callie in her. Where Bridget was frilly and immature, Callie had been independent and practical.

Thinking of Callie now was a bad idea.

Time slowed down. Bridget's foot rose and fell, bringing her a few inches closer to me. Her skirts drew forward, as if of their own accord. Her mouth opened and closed in a giggle that sounded far-off and distorted. And then came the distinctive scent of lemon and ginger.

Everything blurred—

Katherine?

Suddenly, instead of Bridget coming toward me dressed as a bride was the woman who had brought me to this place. Her thick black hair was caught up in a lace veil, revealing her perfect shoulders and neck. The blue cameo gleamed on her neck. She lowered her head demurely, but beneath her long lashes her eyes danced mischievously in my direction. She pursed her lips and I felt my knees weaken.

Did Damon see her, too? I looked askance at my brother, to see if he was thinking or seeing the same thing I was. Whatever compelled me to feel the way I did about Katherine, true love or a vampire's Power, I was still under her spell, haunted by her. But Damon's face was a perfect mask of happiness and love.

Time started back up again. Bridget resumed her place in my sight, smiling excitedly up at me.

And then the girls were before us, and the priest was there, and rings were in our hands.

It was, thankfully, a fairly short ceremony. The priest gave a speech about love and read several nice passages from the Bible that I would have liked in any other circumstance. I wasn't sure whether to pray that the priest go on, and on, and on, and give me as much time as possible before the inevitable, or if he should just hurry up and get it over with.

"If anyone here knows of any impediment why these two couples may not be lawfully joined together in matrimony, you do now confess it."

I looked around the room, hoping someone would stand up and object. Maybe Margaret would speak out, with some sort of proof that *Damon DeSangue* wasn't who he said he was, or that I was some sort of Confederate spy, or . . . The oldest sister shook her head and gritted her teeth, but kept silent. I may have imagined it, but I think her mother's hand had an iron grip on her knee.

Damon went first, marrying the elder bride. I wasn't listening; there seemed to be a dull roar in my ears that was so loud I was surprised no one else could hear it.

What was going to happen when it was over? Would the Sutherlands make it through this night? Would I be forced, on my wedding day, to fight my own brother to the death?

"Repeat after me," the priest finally said. I did as I was told.

"I, Stefan Salvatore, take thee, Bridget Lynn Cupbert Sutherland, to be my wedded wife, to have and to hold, from this day forward, for better, for worse, for richer, for poorer, in sickness and in health, to love and to cherish, till . . . death us do part."

I almost choked, and could only hope that the audience thought I was overwhelmed with emotion.

"I, Bridget Lynn Cupbert Sutherland, take thee, Stefan, to be my wedded husband, to have and to hold, from this day forward, for better, for worse, for richer, for poorer, in sickness and in health, to love and to cherish, till death us do part." She forgot my surname, and from the look in her eyes it was because she was thinking about the night before.

And then there was a ring in my hand. A simple gold band with my and Bridget's initials inscribed on the inside. Precious metal binding me to my fate.

I took Bridget's hand. My voice came out surprisingly

clear and calm. "With this ring, I thee wed, and with my worldly goods I thee endow, in the name of the Father, and of the Son, and of the Holy Ghost." I slipped it on her finger. She squealed in joy.

I kissed her. It was hard and quick, hopefully long enough for the audience to appreciate. Bridget clung to me, trying to make the moment last. She tasted of mint. I felt terrible.

And just like that, I was a married vampire.

The reception was held in a different grand hall. My brother, Lydia, Bridget, and I formed a receiving line by the entrance to thank and greet our guests. Damon put it on a bit, bowing and pretending to know people he didn't. Compelling them into thinking he was an old friend, no doubt. While Bridget showed off her ring, Lydia gave everyone warm kisses or handshakes or smiles, whatever their relationship dictated. She even laughed when Bram tried to snatch a "farewell" kiss. Bridget stood by her side, beaming with what looked like genuine joy.

"Thank you for coming today," I said time and time again, the words tasting like chalk on my tongue. "We're so glad you could come celebrate with us. My thanks for being here today. Pleased to meet you, thank you so much for being here."

"Stefan *Salvatore*?" demanded a matron in an almost unmoving thick gray silk dress and pearls, holding on to my hand for longer than was strictly necessary. She pronounced the *e* at the end of my last name and fixed me with an eye as stony as her skirts.

"Yes, ma'am," I said, giving her as warm a smile as I could.

"Of the *Florentine* Salvatores? Prince Alessandro?"

"I'm not rightly sure, ma'am," I answered, trying to keep my smile. "When my father came to this country he declared himself an American. He didn't keep up with our old relations."

Her eyes widened and her grip on my hand became loose. "An *immigrant*. How charming." She didn't smile and pulled her hand out of my grasp, moving on.

Several hundred people later we finally got to sit down. The bride and groom's table was festooned with palm fronds and garlands of huge flowers, and was covered with every expensive delicacy you could want to eat—or show off that you could afford. There was a seafood appetizer of oysters and other delicacies including Scottish smoked salmon and Russian caviar. Then came a main course that consisted of an absolutely staggering number of dead animals: roast beef, quail, venison, pheasant, woodcock, duck, lamb, roast pork, hot and cold, braised and grilled, minced and sautéed, sliced and in pies.

It was all crowned off by a wedding cake, five tiers of the finest fruitcake covered in fondant and decorated with scrolls, swoops, columns, and sugar birds. The black-jacketed waiters poured glass after glass of champagne, and everyone chatted gaily. But my muscles were tied in knots. The "wedding" was officially over. Damon and I were legally married into the Sutherland family. It was only a matter of time before he began the next phase of his plan—whatever that ended up being.

"Darling, get me a glass of water, would you?" Lydia was asking my brother, touching him tenderly on the cheek.

"In *some* ceremonies, it's the lady's place to love, honor, and *obey*. Shouldn't you be getting one for me, little wife?" he smiled, but in a way I didn't like.

"Of course! Anything for you, dear," Lydia said. "Water, wine . . ."

"Blood?" Damon prompted.

Lydia laughed. "If you wish, it's my command."

Bridget didn't eat any of the expensive repast, leaping up from the table constantly to talk to her friends, holding out her hand and showing off her ring. I spent most of dinner nervously pushing very expensive food around a very expensive plate with a very expensive, very heavy silver fork, never taking my eyes off Damon.

As dessert came out, Bram took pity on me and sat

down in Bridget's place for a moment.

"Congrats, old chap," he said, shaking my hand. "You and Damon snagged two of the best New York has to offer."

I nodded miserably.

"Mr. and Mrs. Sutherland are just terrific. And Margaret . . . well, she's a spitfire, but I trust you'll be able to win her over eventually."

My head snapped up. "Have you noticed anything, er, odd about Margaret?" Bram had known the Sutherlands since he was born. Perhaps he had some insight into what made Margaret able to withstand Damon's charms.

Bram scratched his floppy black curls. "Odd?"

"Yes, she's different from the others. Stronger," I said leadingly.

Bram let out a rueful laugh. "That's for sure. One time when we were younger, I stole her favorite doll to use it as a nurse in a war game with my brother. I swear, the look she gave me! She didn't even have to touch me to send a painful shock through my entire body. Needless to say, I never played with her toys again."

"She was able to hurt you without touching you?" I pressed, trying to put the pieces together.

But just then, Winfield tapped me on the shoulder and nodded toward a back room. Damon came with us, a mock-serious look on his face. As we quietly filed past the guests and down a side corridor, I strained to look out the windows.

Through trees and towers I could see the mighty Hudson and the Palisades, a golden sun shining down on the sparkling river, the green forests, boats and barges parading slowly up and down the water. I almost did feel like a king surveying his countryside, since marrying into this family set me into the top of New York's highest society.

We entered a dark-paneled smoking room, and Winfield immediately set about pouring some ruby-red sherry. Damon pulled out a silver flask and right there in front of Winfield spiked his drink with blood. *Human* blood.

"To marriage eternal," Damon said, raising his glass.

Winfield agreed energetically. "To marriage."

I just nodded and tossed back the drink, hoping the cool liquid would sate my thirst.

"There's a serious matter I need to talk to you lads about." Winfield settled his frame into a large desk chair. Damon leaned forward expectantly. I tensed in my seat, ready for whatever would come next.

"The matter of a dowry."

I squeezed my hands together. Damon grinned, exposing his gleaming canines. He threw himself on to a velvet couch. "Just what I was going to ask you about, Father. You don't mind me calling you that, do you?"

"Not at all, my boy," Winfield said, offering Damon a cigar.

My brother took it, carefully trimming and lighting the end in a matter so professional I wondered where he picked up the habit.

The two sat puffing for a moment, releasing large clouds of smoke into the tiny room. I coughed. Damon, enjoying my discomfort, took the effort to blow a smoke ring my way.

"Now here's the thing. I want you two boys to be able to stand on your own two feet. My girls deserve real men, and if anything should happen to me, I want to make sure they're taken care of."

"Of course," Damon said, out the corner of his mouth, around the cigar.

"I have several mines in Virginia; one is gold. They could use some managing. And then there are the railway shares I've bought into . . ."

My brother widened his eyes. I looked away, unable to bear watching him compel this poor man. "*I would prefer cash*," he said.

"All right, that seems reasonable," Winfield said without pause or even blinking. "An annuity, then? A living salary?"

"*Up front. All of it*," Damon said pleasantly.

"One twentieth of my estate, capital, and holdings, then?" Winfield asked politely.

"*More like a quarter.*"

An automaton, Winfield mindlessly agreed to everything Damon suggested.

But I couldn't figure it out—would this keep Winfield safe? Would Damon just keep him around, ordering whatever he pleased out of him?

"I'm glad you're so concerned about taking care of my girls in the manner to which they have been accustomed," Winfield said, but his voice sounded hollow, as if somewhere some tiny part of his mind knew something was terribly wrong.

The poor man drew out some checks and a pen. In a moment it was done, and Winfield presented me with a check with so many zeroes on it, it was barely readable.

Damon bared his teeth in something that was less a grin than a rictus of victory. He stood up, holding his glass of blood-laced sherry next to me. The smell was intoxicating. It took every ounce of my strength not to leap up and drain the cup.

And then Winfield said the most amazing, banal thing in the world.

"Those checks will take a while to clear," he apologized, unaware of how those eight words might have just saved his life.

Damon glowered, thunderheads in his eyes. It was a look of angry frustration that was famous in Mystic Falls, and something no one wanted to be responsible for causing. It was a dangerous thing to disappoint my brother. He crumpled the check in his hands.

"You didn't mention that before," he growled, waving the sherry under my nose. I stiffened, my thirst making my fangs burn.

"I'm going to have to sell a great deal of my estate, capital, and holdings to get the cash to back this," Winfield answered so plaintively it made me sick.

"*So do it!*" Damon ordered. But I was no longer paying attention. I had to get out of the room. My Power reacted to my hunger—to my anger—and I felt the beginnings of a change.

"I have to . . ." I didn't even bother making up an excuse.

I pushed my way out of the room, past my evil brother and our sad father-in-law, out of the castle, and into the black night where I belonged.

18

There were two hundred blocks between the Richards' mansion and downtown New York City. Just under ten miles. But moving like a vampire isn't like running in a normal sense, especially as I had just drained one of the Richards' goats. If I was a blur to the world, so was the world to me. My head was down as I spent my entire focus on avoiding the obstacles right before me and trying to exhaust myself. Down from the rocky cliffs and heights of Fort Tryon with its cool trees, and through the valley that separated it from the rest of the city. Back into civilization, the unpaved dirt roads that smelled of dust and plants, particularly the tobacco I recognized from my native Virginia.

After enduring a week of waiting and watching and trying to outthink my brother, I just wanted it to all be over.

And now it wasn't.

Damon couldn't kill Winfield until the cash was available, and who knew how long that was going to be. In the meantime I had to stay with Bridget, keep tabs on the Sutherlands, pretend to be happily married, and continue to try and figure out Damon's endgame.

I was caught in a web of guilt; every move of mine stuck another limb deeper. I just wanted to break free.

I wish I could live in solitude. If I had to live out eternity as a vampire, at the very least I could leave no evidence of it. No deaths, no injury, no hurt, no evidence of my unnatural existence at all. I was running from myself, my new self, and could never escape, just as I ran from Damon, my shadow in this endless afterlife.

The scent of nature soon gave way to the reek of sewage and rot that clung to even rich neighborhoods. In the alleyways behind the giant houses, servants dumped slop out into back streets and milk carts left fresh dairy products on back steps. All they would notice was a strange rush of wind, a vacuum that had been created in my passing, a momentary darkening against a brick wall like a cloud had passed over the sun.

In the Garment District my nose was assailed by the harsh tang of chemicals and the singeing of fibers as young women cut, sewed, and dyed cloth in the factories that were beginning to replace the farms in New York City.

Leaning against the fire escape with their sleeves pushed up, small clusters of these young women smoked cigarettes on their precious breaks.

As I tore by one girl, cutting it very close, my tail wind snuffed out her match. I looked back to see her staring, confused, at the feather of smoke.

Soon I was overcome by the smell of human flesh and waste. Of horse manure and flickering gas lamps. Of industry, print and ink and black smog, of the river, briny fish, and finally a fresh breeze. These were the only details of the city I took in, all sounds and sights muted to a roaring black and white. Expensive perfume and flowers. Butchered meat and smoky bacon. Lemon and ginger . . .

I stopped suddenly, in the middle of Washington Square. That was Katherine's perfume.

A hand clasped my shoulder, and I spun around expectantly.

But instead of seeing the dark curls of the woman who had made me, I found myself face-to-face with Damon, who stood there, one eyebrow raised in condescending amusement.

My face fell and I slumped, exhaustion and despair overtaking me. I didn't even bother shaking off his hand. Where was I going to go, really? My brother had followed me all the way up the East Coast. So long as I refused to drink human blood, he would always be stronger, faster than I was. I was only delaying the inevitable by trying to escape whatever he had planned next.

"It's our wedding night, brother. Where are you off to?" Damon's voice was sharp.

Exhausted from my marathon of pain and escape, I just stood there. "I was going to come back."

Damon rolled his eyes. "I'll get us a cab," he said, snapping his fingers. One came over immediately.

"Seventy-third and Fifth," he ordered, through the trap door.

"We're going to the Sutherlands'?" I asked, confused. "Not the Richards'?"

"We're going home," Damon corrected. "And yes, the reception's over. You ran out at the very end."

"What did you tell Bridget?" I couldn't help asking. While I didn't love her, I felt bad about abandoning her at her own wedding. In some ways, it was the worst thing that I could do to a girl like her.

Damon rolled his eyes. "Don't worry. They don't even realize you've gone missing."

"So you haven't killed them yet?"

"Whoever said I was going to kill them?" he asked innocently. "Do you think I'm some kind of monster?"

"Yes," I said.

"Well, I am what you made me," Damon said with a tip of his hat.

"You're not making this any easier," I muttered.

"You must have me mistaken for someone who cares about making your life easier," Damon said, suddenly cold, his eyes flashing.

"You know, you've taken a lot of effort to make sure you stay in my life," I pointed out. "Are you sure it's *just* to make me miserable?"

He stared at me. "What are you getting at?"

"I think you need me, Damon," I growled. "I think that under your anger, you're scared and horrified of what you've become. I am the last link to your human self, the only person who knows who you are. And I'm the only person *for the rest of eternity* who will."

Damon narrowed his eyes at me.

"Brother, *you don't know anything about me*," he hissed.

He threw the door of the cab open and swung himself up and out. A soft *thunk* indicated he had landed on the roof. I stuck my head out the window and looked up.

I watched with horror as Damon picked up the driver and ripped his neck open, sucking only a mouthful or two before throwing him off the cab and on to the street.

"Damon! Stop!" I yelled, but it was too late. I tried to dive out the door, to go after the injured man, but Damon threw an arm out and pushed me back into the carriage as he sped around a corner.

Perched on top of the cab, mouth covered in blood, Damon whipped the horse into a frothing frenzy. And so we two brothers hurled northward, one driving and one being driven, like Satan compelling the damned.

19

By the time we reached the Sutherlands', our horse's lips were covered in foam and its eyes were rolling back until they were ringed with white.

"Not much of a racehorse," he said carelessly, leaping down and giving it a pat on its neck. "Wouldn't surprise me if it dropped dead from the exertion."

I stepped out of the carriage, a putrid smell assaulting my nose as if the Thayers had taken up residence next to a slaughter yard. "I think he may already be dead," I said gingerly. I took a deep breath and steadied myself. I had to be ready for whatever came next, be it Damon taking action against the Sutherlands or having to spend the night with my new bride. If that happened, it would be hard to keep my own promise of no more compelling humans. . . .

Steeling myself, I headed for the door.

"Not so fast, brother," Damon said, putting a hand on my chest. Then he slipped it inside my waistcoat as lightly as a pickpocket, and pulled out the check Winfield had written me. "I'll be needing this," he explained happily.

"Oh yes. Money without the *tracks*," I said bitterly. "Much less obvious than robbing a bank vault. So tell me, what about the cab driver? A dead man in the middle of the road—what about *those* tracks?"

"Him? No one will notice him," Damon said, obviously surprised by my interest. "Look around, Stefan. People die in the streets here all the time. He's no one."

Damon had become the type of vampire who had no problem with killing even when it didn't directly benefit him, and he committed murder at the drop of a hat. When I killed in my first days, it was always for thirst, or self-protection. Not for sport. And never simply for the *kill*.

"Besides, it really, *really* irritated you," he added with a grin. "And isn't that what it's all about?"

He gave a little bow and indicated I should enter our new home first. Looking up at its beautiful gray walls and growling gargoyles, I wished no one had ever invited me in, that I had been forced to remain outside forever, a poor creature relegated to the park.

And then somebody screamed.

Damon and I both rushed in, practically tearing the

door off its hinges in our effort to get through.

Margaret was standing in the living room, white as a sheet, her hand over her mouth. And it was very obvious why.

The entire place was spattered in what my spinning mind could only assume was black paint, until its smell hit my nose with the force of a truck: *blood*. Human blood. Gallons and gallons of it slowly dripping down the walls and congealing in pools on the floor. It threw me off guard, my vampire senses reeling from the sheer quantity.

Damon held one hand over his face, as if trying to stifle the sensations, and pointed with his other hand.

At first all I saw was a pair of stockinged legs askew on the rug, as if someone had too much to drink and fell down. Then I realized they weren't attached to a body.

"No . . ." I whispered, sinking to my knees in horror.

The bodies of Lydia, Bridget, Winfield, and Mrs. Sutherland were scattered around the room in pieces.

The family I had married into to protect, the innocent humans I was trying to keep safe from Damon's psychopathic tendencies, were all dead. But they hadn't just been murdered—they had been torn apart and brutalized.

"What did you do?" I growled at Damon, fury turning my eyes red and beginning the change. "*What did you do?*"

I was going to rip his neck out. It was as simple as that. He was a monster, and I should have killed him long ago, long before he had a chance to destroy other people's lives.

But Damon looked just as shocked as I felt. His ice-blue eyes were wide with unfeigned surprise.

"It wasn't me," he said. Margaret shot him a look that could have killed. The way he spoke it was as if he *could* have been him, just as easily—just not this time.

"I believe you," Margaret said softly, shaking her head in abject grief.

I was surprised. Why, after all the questions, all the glares, all the arguments, *why* did she believe him now? Why, when she—again rightfully—assumed he was just after the money and had fled the moment the documents were dry, did she believe he wasn't the murderer? But oddly I believed him, if for no other reason than the callousness of his tone.

As if she could read my thoughts, Margaret turned her eyes to me. "I can always tell when someone is lying," she said simply. "It's a . . . gift, I suppose."

I thought about what Bram had said—how Margaret had hurt him just by looking at him. I touched my ring, thinking of the witch, Emily, who'd cast a spell over it to protect me from the sun. Was it possible that Margaret had powers, too?

I opened my mouth to ask her, but tears were leaking from her eyes. Now was not the time for an interrogation. Taking a deep breath I rose and went over to what was left of the bodies, trying to discover a clue or reason for the massacre.

The other half of Mrs. Sutherland's body was sprawled on its belly next to the couch. One arm was stretched out, as if she were trying to get up, trying to crawl to her youngest daughter.

Bridget's throat had been torn out and all of her limbs had been snapped in half. Her face was untouched, however. In death she looked like the little girl she really was, the soft rose of her cheeks slowly fading to an icy white, her lips opened slightly as if she were asleep. Her eyes, wide and green and clear as a china doll's, were still open in shock. I gently put my hand over her face and pulled her lids down.

Lydia was frozen with a hand over her face, like an ancient Roman tomb carving, dignified even in death. I turned away from her ruined torso, the white bones of her back sticking through her cracked chest.

Winfield looked like a big, slain animal, a buffalo brought down in its prime. There were surprisingly neat gashes down his side, like something had been trying to butcher him.

Finally, I went over to Margaret and put my arms around her, turning her head so she wasn't staring at the scene of carnage anymore. She clung to me, but stiffened in surprise when my hand brushed the skin on the back of her neck.

After a moment she pulled away. Shock seemed to slowly settle down over her features. She sank into a chair and regarded the room again, this time with a blank face.

"They were like this when I arrived," she began slowly. "I stayed at the Richards' longer than everyone else, looking for the two of you, trying to find someone who had seen you leave. Bram and Hilda and the usual gang had left earlier, planning some silly antics for your wedding night. A shivaree or something. I just assumed you two took off for Europe with your dowry."

"Europe," Damon said thoughtfully. I glared at him.

"The door was open," she continued, "and the stench . . ."

We fell into silence. I didn't know what to say or do. In ordinary, human circumstances, my first move would have been to get Margaret away from the house and call for help.

"Did you call for the police?" I asked suddenly.

Margaret met my gaze. "Yes. They'll be here soon. And they'll think it was you, you know."

"It wasn't," Damon repeated.

She nodded, not bothering to look at him. Her skin was milky pale, as if some of the life had gone out of her when her family had died. "I know, but you are not innocent, either."

"No, no, we are not," Damon said in a distant voice,

looking at Lydia's cold body. For a moment, his features softened and he looked almost like a human in mourning. Then, he shook his head, as if snapping himself out of a reverie. "Margaret, I'm sorry for your loss," he said perfunctorily. "But Stefan and I must run."

"Why should I leave with you?" I challenged, the blood making my head spin, my thoughts whirling dizzily in my brain.

"Fine, stay here, get arrested."

I turned to Margaret. "Are you going to be all right?"

She gave me a look as if I was mad. "My entire family is dead."

Her voice quavered on the edge of sanity. I put my hand out and touched her shoulder, wishing I could say or do something. No one deserved this. But words wouldn't bring her family back.

As Damon and I turned to go, the telltale *clip clop* of a police wagon pulling up in front of the house sounded, along with the firm orders of a chief directing his men.

"Out the back," I said. Damon nodded and we ran through the dining room and kitchen to the door that opened on the courtyard. My hand was just about to touch the doorknob when Damon grabbed me, finger to his mouth. He pressed himself up against the wall, indicating I should do the same. My predator's senses picked up what Damon had already figured out: There was a man, no, a pair of men, waiting silently outside with guns drawn, exactly prepared for us to escape that way.

"I'll just quickly dispose of them," Damon said.

"No! Upstairs," I whispered. "Window."

"Fine." Damon sighed, and the two of us started to creep quietly up the servants' staircase.

An explosive *bang* from the front hall made us freeze in our tracks.

"You, upstairs, you and you, to the parlor!" A stern voice was barking orders. From the sounds of footsteps, an entire fleet of policemen was beginning to sweep through the house.

Damon and I gave up any attempt at being quiet, storming up the stairs as fast as we could. There was a casement window at the top, which he threw open triumphantly, prepared to jump to freedom.

Below, in the side yard, a dozen armed policeman stood, aiming rifles at the building. And with his drama, Damon had neatly alerted them all to our presence.

Bullets began to fly.

Though they would not kill us, they would slow us down. I threw myself to the floor, feeling the sting of lead graze my neck.

"Coal chute," I suggested. Without bothering to wait for an answer I streaked back downstairs with vampiric speed, my brother close behind. Police now swarmed all over the rooms on the main floor, but even those who caught a glimpse of us running to the cellar didn't quite know what they saw: blurry shadows, a trick of the eye.

The darkness of the basement proved no problem for us, and in a split second we were in the coal room, behind the furnace. I forced open the tiny slanted door that led to the driveway and leaped out, turning to give my brother a hand.

And that's when I felt the gun at my neck.

I turned around slowly and raised my hands. A small crowd of New York's finest stood there, along with most of the neighborhood, who had come to watch the manhunt.

Damon and I could, with little difficulty, have taken them all. And it looked like my brother was itching for a fight.

I shook my head, whispering, "We'll draw far more attention resisting arrest right now." The truth was, it would be far easier to escape later, when we didn't have a crowd gawking at us. Damon knew it as well as I did.

Damon sighed a dramatic sigh and pulled himself out of the chute, leaping neatly to the ground.

An officer strode forward bravely—but only once his men had our arms behind our backs and jostled us a bit, letting us know who was in charge.

"You two are under arrest for grand larceny, murder, and anything else I can find that will have you hanging from a tree in Washington Square for the death of the Sutherlands," the officer said through even, square teeth.

They dragged us out, pushing more than was necessary. With shoves and a final kick each we were thrown into the back of a paddy wagon, and then the door was slammed behind us.

"They were good people," the chief hissed in Damon's face, through the bars.

Damon shook his head back and forth. "I've had better," he whispered to me.

Through the bars of the wagon I stared back at the house I'd called home for the past week. Margaret stood framed in the doorway, her black hair stark against the glowing lights of the house. Tears streamed down her cheeks as she said something so softly that even my sensitive ears barely heard it.

"Whoever did this will pay."

20

he New York Halls of Justice and House of
Detention was a slablike stone structure that
rose heavily from the street like an old tomb-
stone. The interior was a portrait in gray, with grim-faced
policemen and haggard criminals.

And us.

Vampires caught in a human system for a bloody crime
we didn't commit. The twistedness of it all was remarkable, but it did nothing to alleviate our current situation.

With our hands tied behind our backs, a young policeman marched Damon and me up several flights of worn
wooden stairs and into the chief's office. He commanded
a small square of the larger floor. Sketches of wanted men
lined his walls, one man's eye struck through with a large
nail. The chief himself was a grizzled veteran with a full

black beard, except for where a smooth, diagonal scar cut through his skin.

He looked at our rap sheet and let out a low whistle. "The whole Sutherland family? That'll be in the papers tonight."

I flinched at hearing such insensitivity coming from the lips of a normal human. What sort of monsters did he deal with that the death of an entire family was no more than a news item?

"We didn't do it," I said.

"No, of course you didn't," the chief said gruffly, running a finger along his scar. "No one who ends up here has ever done it. But the courts will get it sorted out, and everyone will get what they deserve."

We were unceremoniously dumped into a holding cell that was larger than the entire one-person jail back home, where Jeremiah Black spent many a night sleeping off his drunken stupor. I never expected to see the inside of a cell myself.

"*We didn't do it*," Damon whined, imitating me and shaking his head, as soon as the guard left. "Could you make us sound any more ridiculous?"

"What, are you afraid of us coming off as sissies?" I asked. "Would you rather I just bared my fangs at him?"

A rasping chuckle came from the corner of the cell, where another prisoner sat slumped against the wall. His hair receded from his forehead in a deep V and he had the arms of a dockworker.

"Nice clothes," he said with malicious growl, eyeing our formal suits and clean-shaven cheeks. "What are *you* in for, rich boys?"

"Killing a family," Damon answered without pause. "You?"

"Beatin' in the heads of the likes of you," he answered back just as quickly, cracking his knuckles.

He took a swing at Damon, but my brother reached up and, with hands faster than the human eye, deflected the blow, and pushed the man against the wall with a loud crack.

The giant didn't so much topple as just crumple straight down, falling into an unconscious puddle around his own feet. None of the officers came running, and I wondered if fighting in the cells was an ordinary occurrence.

Damon sighed as he stepped around the man. He sat down on the floor in a moment of exhaustion that was almost human, almost like the old brother I used to know. "Why is it we *always* end up locked behind bars with each other?"

"Well, at least this time you're not being starved," I answered drily.

"Nope. No chance in that," Damon said. His eyes surveyed the police standing on the other side of our bars, taking in each person. Then he leaned his head up against the wall and gave the peeling paint a grudging sniff. "And I think there's more than a chance that there are a couple of rats in here for you, too."

I sighed, sliding down the wall and sitting next to him. I did not understand this new Damon. His shifts in mood were frightening. One moment he was the soulless vampire who killed without remorse, the next he was someone who seemed like my old childhood companion again.

"What's the plan?" I asked.

"You're looking at it," he said, getting up and indicating the dead man at our feet. "*Guard!* Man down in here."

When the guard approached and saw the body on the ground he seemed annoyed, but not surprised. The guard didn't lean too close—he had survived long enough to know not to. But it was close enough. Damon flared his eyes.

"*Forget we were ever here. Forget what we look like. Forget who brought us in, our names, and everything about us.*"

"Who's us?" the guard asked, hypnotized but slow on the uptake.

"The man I came in with," Damon snapped, pointing at me. The guard nodded faintly. "*Forget everything about us. And then—send over the other guard, all right?*"

The guard wandered back to his post, somewhat dizzily

at first, then cocked his head as if he had just remembered something. He went to one of the guards on patrol and pointed at the jail cell. Not at Damon, *through* Damon. It was like Damon didn't exist anymore in his reality.

"One down," Damon muttered. He looked tense. Again I wondered how many people he really could control at once.

The second guard approached. He had a scar across his face that twisted one eye shut, and he smacked his billy club as he walked. But before Damon could compel him, he said the absolute last thing we expected.

"Your lawyer is here."

I looked at my brother. He looked back at me in equal surprise. He raised an eyebrow as if to say: *Did you arrange this somehow?*

I very slightly shook my head. Damon straightened his shoulders as a clang sounded and the door to the stockade opened. The smell of rotten eggs and death filled the room as another man walked in—the lawyer.

He was huge. Larger than the prisoner Damon had knocked out, with long arms and a huge chest. His hands were monstrous, with stubby fingers that gripped a leather portfolio.

He came into the room slowly, with the careful tread of someone or something too large and dangerous for its surroundings, like the pace of a panther around its tiny circus cage.

His clothing was of a foreign cut, comfortable, rich linen and silk that allowed his massive body to move easily beneath its folds.

And his eyes . . .

They were small and blue, but not the clear blue of my brother's. They were mottled, milky almost, and too ancient for the rest of his body, moving quickly but incorrectly, like a bird's or a lizard's gaze, but with a powerful intelligence behind it.

This man was not human.

He didn't feel like a vampire, not exactly. But there was something just below his surface waiting for a chance to explode. The Power radiating from him was greater than anything I had experienced. And my instincts told me that even though he had come under the auspices of being our lawyer, this man was not here to help us.

He surveyed us in the jail cell and smiled slightly.

"You may go," he said to the guard behind him. His voice didn't even rise, but quietly reverberated in a way that carried to the far end of the empty holding cells. And yet they went. Quickly, and with something like relief on their faces.

We were left alone with this beast.

"Good evening, gentlemen," he said, smiling in a way that made me sick.

"Who are you?" Damon asked, clearly trying to sound bored. But I could hear the fear in his voice.

"Who am I?" the man repeated in a heavy accent. "Does it help to know the name of the one who will kill you? It didn't seem any comfort to your wives."

The words fell like stones to the floor, heavy and final. The man casually put a giant hand up to rest on a bar.

"You killed the Sutherlands," I whispered.

"Yes." He smiled and pursed his lips. "It was fun."

"You tore them apart like paper dolls," I said, even though I knew he could tear me apart, too, could scatter my limbs like the petals that had lined my wedding altar. "You . . . *broke* them."

"Young vampire, you must know the hunger of the beast," he said with a smile that wasn't at all amused. "There are other hungers, for other things, that once awoken cannot rest until they are satisfied."

The whites of the man's eyes glowed red, and there was a hush in the air, like great Power was being summoned. I could practically smell the fear coiling off Damon in large strips.

But I began to grow angry.

Rage boiled in my stomach and shot out through my body. This man had butchered an innocent family and *enjoyed* it. This was what my new life as a vampire meant—layers and layers of evil, and even more horror and destruction, just when I felt I had reached the very bottom.

"Why?" I demanded, coming forward as far as the bars would let me. "What did they ever do to you?"

"*Why?*" the beast asked. He leaned forward, mocking my bravado. As he neared, mere centimeters from my face, a sickening stench of old blood and decay swept over me. It was like a thousand years of death and dismemberment followed him around, a trophy from each corpse he was responsible for.

"*Recompense.*" He said each syllable carefully.

"Recompense?" I echoed.

He bared his teeth. "Yes, recompense. For taking Katherine. And destroying any chance to break the curse."

Katherine? What did she have to do with all of this, with this abomination in front of us? With the Sutherlands? And what curse?

I looked over at Damon. She had always shared more details of her life, of being a vampire, with him. But my brother was wide-eyed and gaping like a fish, even more stunned by hearing her name than I was.

I thought about the blissful, ignorant weeks I spent as her slave and lover, never imagining that she would lead me straight into hell.

The man backed up a few steps, including Damon in his foul stare.

"Yes, you understand now," he said, nodding. But we didn't.

"I—" Damon began to speak.

"*SILENCE!*" the man roared. Suddenly he was pressed up against the bars, a blackened fingernail inches from Damon's throat. "Do you dare deny it?"

With a chilling deliberateness, he pushed an iron bar aside like it was a curtain. The metal screamed in agony. In a flash of darkness he had stepped through, and wrapped a giant hand around each of our throats.

"You took Katherine. I take your new life from you. An eye for an eye, as you people are fond of saying. Right?"

"I . . . don't know what you're talking about," I said, choking.

The monster threw back his head and laughed.

"*Of course you don't.*" He snapped his head back, suddenly fixing me with his eyes and a sneer on his lips. He didn't believe me. "Katherine *never* mentioned Klaus?"

Even after her death, Katherine continued to haunt us. I looked over at Damon. There was a pained, heartbroken look on his face. It was gone in an instant, but for that one moment I thought I saw through to my old brother. He was shocked by the fact that Katherine, the love of his life, had been involved with a creature as heartless as the one that stood before us. I felt for him.

Unbidden, half a dozen images of Katherine came to my mind. Her amber eyes that commanded attention. Her long black hair hanging in waves around her neck, as if she had just done something that might have disheveled it. Her tiny waist and mischievous smile. She had been irresistible. And Damon and I weren't the only ones to have felt her pull.

The man tightened his grip on my throat, and I could hear the groaning of vertebrae. In a moment we would be on the floor, our necks snapped as easily as that of the prisoner Damon had killed.

Then suddenly I was free. Damon fell to the ground beside me, also released from the stony grip that held him.

From outside the cell, the monster smiled viciously.

"I will see you two later," he promised.

And then, almost as an afterthought, he used a delicate finger to push the jail bars back into place.

"And remember, I am always watching."

amon and I remained in the cell for several minutes after the man left, too stunned to even contemplate escaping. The guards didn't come back in with the keys. I didn't blame them.

I cursed, slamming the bars. It seemed that no matter what I decided to do, which way I turned, things got worse. And the Sutherlands . . . they had just been innocent bystanders, swept up in the path of destruction just because they were at the wrong place at the wrong time. While my brother didn't actively cause their deaths, he was no less responsible. I turned on him, ready to tear him apart.

And then I saw the look on his face.

Damon's eyes had glazed over and he leaned against the wall for support. He'd worn the same dazed expression for weeks after he'd woken up as a vampire and discovered that Katherine was dead.

"What was that?" he whispered, finally looking at me.

But I had no idea what *that* was. All I knew was that *it* was more powerful, more dangerous, more deadly than any creature I'd ever encountered. Anger at my brother drained away and something like exhaustion set in. "I'm not sure, though I think he left me a message," I said, remembering the bloody scrawl on the side of the Sutherlands' home. "But what was that about Katherine? What *was* he to her?"

Damon shrugged. "I have no idea. She never told me about that . . . thing."

"He said we *took her from him*. What the hell does that mean? What *curse* is he talking about? Did Emily cast a spell on someone?" I said. I began to pace, my mind racing.

"I'm guessing it means he believes we killed her. Which *you* did, brother," Damon said.

In a pique, Damon sat down, stretched his legs out, and put his hands behind his head, pillowing it against the stone. I would get no more answers out of him.

I slid down against the bars and buried my head in my hands, thinking of my time with Katherine. Had she ever said anything about her past? Let anything slip? But I had been so completely under her thrall that it was impossible to know what had been real and what she had compelled me to believe. Though I remembered biting her, I didn't have any memory of her feeding me her blood. But she must have often, as I had enough of her blood in my system to come back as a vampire after my father shot me. In a funny way, Katherine had *made* me. We were almost like her children.

My mind snagged. "Did Katherine ever tell you about her sire?" I asked, putting words to a horrible thought forming in my mind. "The vampire who made her?"

Damon looked up at me, shocked out of his sulk. "You think . . . ?"

I nodded.

Damon leaned back and knocked his head against the wall. He had been genuinely in love with Katherine. I wondered if meeting Katherine's maker made our little tryst in Mystic Falls seem like a speck in the vastness of eternity.

"I suppose we should call a guard over and compel him to free us," he said tiredly.

A sound of commotion from the lobby stopped us. There were muffled thuds, like bodies hitting the floor.

There was a scream. It was high-pitched and hard to tell whether it came from a woman or a man, so great was the pain. Then came the grating sound of a desk being moved, and what might have been a wooden chair being shattered against the wall.

I stood. So did Damon.

Damon and I glanced at each other. The pocket watch Winfield had given me ticked loudly in the sudden silence.

The door to the stockade opened once again and in came a girl wearing men's trousers and black suspenders, a long blond braid over her shoulder.

"Lexi!" I gasped.

"I'm growing tired of bailing you boys out," she said as she shook the key at us. "I should leave you in there over-night, teach you a lesson about making trouble," she joked.

I reached through the bars to grab her free hand. "I've never been happier to see anyone."

"I don't doubt it," Lexi said drily, but a small smile curved the edges of her lips.

Damon rolled his eyes. "We were just about to free our-selves, thank you very much."

"I don't doubt that, either. Just figured I'd speed up the escape," she said. Her nose twitched, and her flat tone indicated she didn't entirely approve of his existence. The last time she'd seen him, he'd just gotten through killing Callie and was starting in on me.

"So did you knock out the entire precinct?" Damon asked, straightening the shoulders of his jacket.

Lexi undid the final lock on the door. The door sprang open and I rushed to hug her. "No, only some of them. The rest I compelled. Some of us don't like needless violence—or messes that need to be explained later," she said into my shoulder. I released her and she motioned us toward the door. "Now let's get out of here before anyone else shows up."

"I always cover my tracks," Damon said defensively as we rushed through the door of the containment area and into the front offices. Several policemen sat at their desks, poring over ledgers, oblivious to the two prisoners escaping and the general state of disarray. Desks had been pushed aside, among the splintery remains of what had once been a chair, and the man who had sat there was lying on the floor, a rivulet of blood leaking from his head. But his eyes were open and he appeared to be whispering some word over and over again.

"Strong-willed, that one," Lexi said.

"How were you able to find us?" I asked, following her down the stairs.

"A mysterious Italian count with black hair and ice-blue eyes and a flair for the dramatic sweeps into the New York social scene and very quickly marries the most eligible society girl?" she said, rolling her eyes. "They ran your picture in the social pages."

Damon at least had the grace to look sheepish.

"*I always cover my tracks*," she mimicked. "There are a lot of ways to live rich and powerfully as a vampire . . . none of which involve *sweeping into the New York social scene . . .*"

". . . and marrying the most eligible society girl. Fair

enough," Damon conceded. "At least I did it with style."

We exited the prison, and the cold evening air washed over me. The stars were just beginning to flicker in the night sky, and the gaslights cast a warm glow over the street. It was a beautiful night, the like of which Bridget, Lydia, Winfield, and Mrs. Sutherland would never enjoy again—all because of me, Damon, and Katherine.

I only came to New York to escape. Escape Damon, memories of Callie, vampires, Mystic Falls, Katherine . . . and yet it all still followed me like an onerous shadow. I knew then that I'd never escape my past, not fully. Such dark things don't fade with time—they merely reverberate through the centuries.

I could only hope that Margaret was safe somewhere, away from the hell-beast that had violently murdered her entire family.

Once we had put several blocks between us and the police precinct, we stopped in the shadows of a bare maple tree. "Well, thanks for the rescue—not that I couldn't have done it myself, eventually," Damon said. "And now, I think I'm ready for a drink. *Adieu, mes amis,*" he saluted us, and spun on his heel, disappearing into the night.

"Good riddance," Lexi muttered.

"What now?" I asked.

"You heard the man. Let's go for a drink," she said, grinning, and put her arm in mine. I walked with Lexi, but it felt wrong, somehow, to be able to go on with my existence so casually knowing that the Sutherlands had been murdered, and it had been partly my doing. What would I tell Margaret? She deserved to know some version of the truth, despite the fact that there would be no justice here. Creatures like the one who killed her family did not suffer consequences for their actions. Human lives were much shorter than vampire lives, but that didn't make them less valuable. In fact, it made their lives more precious.

"So catch me up," she said, squeezing my arm and pulling me out of my dark thoughts. "What's been going on since you left our fair city?"

"I got married today," I said.

Her eyes widened.

"Now I *really* do need a drink," she declared. "Stefan Salvatore, you are going to be the death of me. I have heard of a lovely new place that gets its vodka straight from St. Petersburg and freezes it in a fancy little ice-bottle. . . ."

She prattled on, leading me through what I had thought was *my* city, but New York with Lexi was an entirely different animal. Whereas I'd stuck to the shadows and back alleys, Lexi knew her way around glittering nightlife. Soon we came to what looked like an elegant private club. Thick red carpets covered every square inch of the floor, and gold, black, and red lacquer covered everything else, including a giant carving of a firebird that hung from the ceiling.

A maître d' came up, and after one look at Lexi, ushered us over to the most extravagant booth. It had velvet and cloth-of-gold pillows with far too many tassels to be perfectly comfortable. The strains of a piano filtered from the next room over, and I understood why she'd chosen this bar—Lexi always asked Hugo, a member of her vampire family in New Orleans, to play piano for her.

"Married?" she said as soon as we were settled in and she had ordered us something.

The image of the Sutherlands' bloody bodies scorched my vision for a moment.

"How did you know where we were, really?" I asked, changing the subject. News didn't travel that fast unless it was about the war. It still should have taken her at least a week to get from Louisiana to New York, whether by train or vampiric speed.

"I set one of my friends after Damon. I worried about you," she admitted, a sheepish look on her face. "I know you can take care of yourself, but Damon is dangerous, Stefan, and I don't want anything to happen to you."

The waiter came over with our drinks. As promised, the bottle was encased in a block of bluish ice with flowers and herbs pressed inside, as fresh as the day they were frozen. I couldn't help touching a fingertip to a blossom that was near the surface, and feeling the ridge of rime that separated it from my skin. A human's heat would have melted the ice. A vampire's flesh was colder, kept in a similar state of perpetual frozen perfection.

The waiter poured us each a shot in goblets carved from solid green malachite.

I put my hand over hers. "Thank you, Lexi. For everything you've done. I can never repay you."

"No, you can't," she said cheerfully. "But you can start by telling me *everything*. As I said before: *married*?"

So I told her about my discovery of Bridget and being inducted into the Sutherland household, and Damon's insane plans. She giggled and gasped at every detail. I guess from an outsider's perspective, particularly a much older vampire, Damon's machinations might seem mild in comparison.

"Oh, oh my God," she said, unable to stop laughing. "A *double wedding*? You and Damon together? And no one ate the flower girl?" She waved the waiter over for another bottle of vodka. "Oh, how I *wish* I was there. Stefan! I didn't even get you anything. . . ."

I smiled, wishing I could just sit there and continue to watch her laugh. But I had to finish the tale.

"Are you *sure* it wasn't Damon?" she asked quietly, when I told her of the Sutherlands' murders.

"There are a lot of things I can't predict about him," I admitted. "I had no idea he would actually follow me to the ends of the earth just to make my life miserable—even after he murdered Callie. But I'm positive he had nothing to do with the slaying—he was just as surprised as I was.

And he has not been one to hide his evil acts. Besides, Margaret even believed him and apparently she has a sixth sense about these things," I said.

"New York City isn't exactly the ends of the earth," she said, but this time there was no humor in her voice. "But it's an odd coincidence that some other monster would set his sights on the very same family that you did."

"It wasn't a coincidence at all."

Lexi's face went ashen as I recounted what the lawyer had said. A look I had never seen before on her crossed her pretty face—dread.

"Describe him to me," she ordered.

"He was huge. Blond hair, blue eyes. He seemed older than time," I said, struggling to express the ancient menace I felt. "Evil. Just pure darkness radiating out of him."

"Did he . . . did he have an accent?" she asked hesitantly, as if she already knew the answer.

"Yes. I thought it was just part of whatever he was. But it could have been Polish or Russian. He said something about someone named Klaus?"

Lexi thumped the underside of the table with her fist and looked away.

"Who was it, Lexi?" I demanded. I needed to know. If he was going to be my executioner, if he was the one who had murdered the Sutherlands, at the very least I would get to know who my enemy was.

"He mentioned Klaus?" she asked, speaking more into her glass than to me. "Everyone knows about him. He was one of the first vampires."

A hush seemed to descend over the restaurant, and the gas lamps flickered. I clutched my glass of vodka.

"He is directly descended from Hell. Any piece of good, any sense of morality, anything at all that keeps you and me—and even Damon—from becoming a completely twisted, raving monster of pure evil—none of that is in him. There is nothing human about him. He has minions, other old ones who do his bidding. No one's ever seen Klaus—or at least lived to tell about it!"

I digested this horrifying information, wrapping my hands around my glass. "This . . . thing said we took *Katherine*."

Lexi paled. "If she was important to Klaus and he believes that you and your brother are responsible for what happened to her, you're in serious trouble."

"He mentioned a curse. Do you know what he's talking about?"

Lexi drummed her fingers against the table, her brow furrowing. "Curse? Many vampires consider being confined to wander at night a curse, but I don't know what Katherine had to do with that."

"Do you think he . . . did he turn *her* into a vampire?" I asked.

"That's irrelevant," Lexi said. "It's doesn't matter how or why he cares about her—just that he does. You have your own fate to worry about."

I ran my hands through my hair, frustrated. Once again Katherine had found a way to insert herself into my life and create havoc. While I felt guilty about what had happened to Katherine, I still blamed her for destroying my family, for turning my life into the mess it was now.

Katherine had been nothing but selfish. She'd toyed with me and Damon, when Damon fell in love with her and I . . . well, was falling in lust with her, not once did she think about the possible dangers for us. That we would die, that our brotherhood would be severed irreparably, that her sire might eventually catch up to her, hell-bent on revenge.

"I have to get rid of him," I said.

Lexi shook her head. "You're not 'getting rid' of anything that old and powerful, my young stripling. You're just a babe—and on top of that, your diet of rodents and birds hasn't exactly strengthened you. You and your brother working together couldn't defeat him. *I* couldn't take him on."

"Well, what do I do?" I demanded, my voice taking on a hard, determined edge. I had just been letting everything that had come along in my life control me—Damon and his stupid plans, getting married. . . . It was time I acted.

Lexi rubbed her temples. "The best you can hope for right now is to figure out what his plans are—and then avoid them. You will need to live long enough to figure out a way to vanquish this old one, before he has a chance to tell Klaus where you are."

I nodded, thinking. "We need to go back to the mansion."

Lexi opened her mouth, but I put up my hand. "I know—but maybe he left something behind."

Lexi squared her jaw. "I'll go with you. My senses are more finely tuned than yours."

"You don't need finely tuned senses to catch the scent of Hell," I told her, "but I appreciate the help."

23

We hailed a carriage heading uptown—Lexi told me I needed to save my strength for whatever came next—and got out without bothering to pay. This was what life was like for one such as Lexi, powerful and simple in her wants and desires. She didn't need any intricate, crazy plans for amassing wealth. She could compel anyone to do anything she asked, and life was incredibly easy.

It was tempting, especially the aspect that was non-violent. No one was hurt in any of her activities, except financially.

Lexi must have read my thoughts because she grinned at me and waggled her eyebrows. "You should stick with me, my friend. Life like this can be sweet, not a curse," she offered.

I shook my head, smiling. "Thanks, but as you keep saying, I have my own path."

By the time we made it to the Sutherland mansion, its windows were dark and already draped in festoons of black crepe. In the strange half-light of the early hour, dew sparkled eerily off the matte cloth. The house was cordoned off.

I gently forced the lock. Neither Lexi nor I made any noise until we came into the living room, when she gave a gasp.

The coroners had removed the bodies but not done any cleanup work. The vast amounts of blood from their ripped-up bodies had seeped into the carpet and stained the marble floors beneath. Dark black splatters of dried blood covered the walls, matching the crepe outside.

"My god," Lexi whispered. "He *massacred* them."

I fell back into a chair, overwhelmed with guilt. It hadn't been long since I had discovered the poor family here, their bodies still warm with rapidly fleeting life. Backward and backward my thoughts ran, remembering the things I had done wrong, all of which had led up to this sad climax.

If I hadn't run away from the reception . . .

If hadn't gone along with my brother's plans to begin with . . .

If I hadn't saved Bridget . . .

If I hadn't fled to New York . . .

If I hadn't made Damon drink blood to complete his transformation . . .

"This is my fault," I moaned.

I put my head in my hands. The trail of blood and death that wasn't even of my own devising followed me like a curse.

"No, it's Damon's," Lexi corrected promptly. "And Klaus's."

"I should never have come here. . . . I should have stayed as far away from humans as possible."

"Hey." Lexi walked over to me, kneeling down and looking up into my face. She put a hand on my chin, forcing me to look back at her. "*You* didn't do this. Klaus did—he ordered this. And *you* had no intention of marrying into this family. That was Damon's idea. You told me yourself—he threatened to kill that roomful of people if you didn't go along. *I* would have killed *him* at that point, but he's not my brother."

I gazed into her dark eyes. "I've done so much wrong."

She bit her lower lip. "You made mistakes in the past. Bad ones. But you know that, and were doing your best to correct them, or at least avoid them in the future. That's why I am here, Stefan. You're worth saving."

A pain that had nothing to do with thirst made my throat ache. "Lexi, please . . ."

"I can see into your heart, Stefan," she said softly. "I don't just appear out of the blue to save *any* vampire. You're different. And someday, maybe, you'll know that. And part of your curse will be over."

She leaned forward and pressed her lips against my cheek. I could feel the soft flutter of her eyelashes as she closed her eyes against my face.

"Come on," she said, backing up and chucking me under the chin. "We have work to do. I'll look around down here. You go get whatever things of yours the police haven't confiscated. I think you're moving out of this town for a while."

Between one breath and the next, between a trick of the light and the deepest shadow, she had changed. Sunny, friendly Lexi now had bloodred eyes and black veins around her face. Fangs glistened in what little light there was. She was in full predator mode, hunting for the slightest sign of the vampire. Even though she was just an older version of what I was, seeing her that way still sent a chill down my body. Lurking just beneath our skin, the monster was always ready to come out.

With a heavy heart I plodded up the grand, dark wood staircase. There was no need to be completely silent; the few servants who remained were in their quarters in a distant wing, far away from the death and mess. I could hear their overloud voices, their discussions of prospects and other households—all desperate attempts to fend off the darkness that their employers had slipped into so suddenly.

I wondered what Margaret was doing, vowing to get word to her about Klaus and his vendetta. She was probably in her own home with her husband, mourning her sisters and parents. Which was harder? To be dead, or to live with the memory of the dead? As a vampire, I would never know the former, but always experience the latter.

I soon reached my room, where a night ago Bridget had thrown herself at me. I smelled traces of the violet perfume she had doused herself with. It had infiltrated my pillow and sheets. So much more childish than Katherine's scent, the subtle, alluring, complicated mix of citrus and spice. . . .

I took a valise—another gift from Winfield, planning for our honeymoon, I suppose—and threw the few things I considered mine into it. My old clothes, some spare change, my journal. I flipped to an old page where I'd written about Katherine.

September 8, 1864

She is not who she seems. Should I be surprised? Terrified? Hurt?

It's as if everything I know, everything I've been taught, everything I've believed in my past seventeen years is wrong.

I can still feel where she kissed me, where her fingers grasped my hands. I still yearn for her, and yet the voice of reason is screaming in my ears: you cannot love a vampire!

If I had one of her daisies, I could pluck the leaves and let the flower choose for me. I love her . . . I love her not . . . I . . .

I love her.

I do. No matter the consequences.

Is this what following your heart is? I wish there was a map or a compass to help me find my way. But she has my heart and that above all else is my North Star . . . and that will have to be enough.

I snapped the book shut, curling my lip at my foolishness. Downstairs was the present reality and thinking about the past did no good. I threw the book into the valise and went downstairs.

But instead of finding Lexi there to greet me, there was emptiness and a horrible, familiar scent.

Death and decay.

A faint breeze whistled through broken wood; the back

door was left wide open. I shivered despite myself. The silence, Lexi's absence, howled like a banshee.

A single piece of paper, the size of a ticket, fluttered on the floor. I picked it up, feeling dread prickle my skin.

All it said was: PAYMENT NUMBER TWO —LUCIUS.

24

November 13, 1864

I am cursed. It is obvious now. Maybe that's what being a vampire means. Maybe tragedy and evil come with the hunger and the fangs; it isn't just having to live off human blood. It is the unending aloneness, being cut off from real life and from real relationships. Death will always be there to separate me from those I loved.

There is a scroll of names in my head, and the list kept getting longer every day. Rosalyn was the first to die because of me. Katherine couldn't stand that I was engaged, so she killed the girl. Even Katherine's blood was on my hands.

Though she came into my and my brother's lives and turned them upside down. She died as a result of my actions. I should never have tried to reason with my father, never tried to convince him of a different viewpoint. As soon as he confided in me about the vampire hunt, I should have done everything I could to get Katherine out of town.

Pearl. She, too, could have escaped. I don't know exactly what her story was, but she seemed far more peaceable than Katherine.

Alice the barmaid.

All the humans I fed on in New Orleans. Too many to name, even if I had bothered learning their names. They were just unlucky folk who accidentally crossed my path when I was hungry or needed something.

Callie. She died because I was stupid enough to think that she would be rewarded for helping out two vampires.

The Sutherlands.

Bridget, Lydia, Mrs. Sutherland, and Winfield. A normal family who just happened to catch the attention of one insane, vengeful vampire.

And now Lexi. Lexi should have stayed in New

*Orleans in her hostel for the undead, safe in her
own world where she could continue her own version of doing good.*

*She will be the next to die unless I figure out
how to save her.*

*I have spent too much time in New York
bemoaning my fate, moping, feeling cursed. By
standing idly by, by complaining, I am letting evil
occur all around me. Now is the time for action,
for justice. I must channel my loneliness and
despair into rage. I must stop being a coward, as
I've always been, in both life, when I let my father
bully me into a marriage I didn't want, and in
death, when I've allowed Damon to torture me
and kill the people I love.*

*Never again will I let others bend me to their
will. From now on I will fight.*

And I will free Lexi, if it is the last thing I do.

I crumpled the piece of paper in my fist, growling with
anger. *How had he taken her?* I hadn't heard a thing, even
with my vampire senses. The servants, a couple of mice
and rats in the walls, but nothing else. The vampire Lucius
had come in complete silence and managed to seize—or
disable—Lexi before she was able to cry out. What speed,
what Power this beast must have!

But for all of the vampire's ancientness, for all that he was a "direct descendant from Hell," for all of the monster he was, he had, with that single piece of paper, revealed one very human weakness about himself. He had a very petty need to *gloat*. If Damon were in his place, I would have come downstairs and seen Lexi dead on the floor. But the beast wanted me to know that everyone around me was in danger, to scare me before he killed me.

Now there was only one thing on my mind. If Lexi was still alive, it was my duty to go after her and save her. And if she wasn't alive . . . it was my right and pleasure to kill Klaus's foot soldier. This I swore.

What was it he had said in the prison? *An eye for an eye.* He took something valuable from me and Damon, our wives and their family, because we had taken Katherine from him. But the Sutherlands were human, of no importance and very easily disposed of. His beloved Katherine died in a church fire.

What if . . .

The words struggled to the surface of my brain.

What if he planned on killing Lexi the same way?

Suddenly I felt like I had a chance again. But which church? There had to be hundreds in the city.

I ran outside. The smell of decay hung heavy in the air, as though Lucius had unwittingly laid a path for me. I followed it south, feeling as though I were gaining strength with each step that brought me closer to where Lexi might be—and who I *should* be. I had tried to stay away from humans, and that hadn't worked. I had tried living with them, with disastrous results. But I had never tried a more moderate path. I would never be human, but I could help them, as I'd helped Bridget that night in the park. I could never live among humans, but I could find companionship among humans like Mrs. Sutherland and vampires like Lexi. Those ties would tether me to this world and keep me honest.

I ran past a brick town house and grabbed a pigeon in midflight from the air, tearing into its neck for extra fuel. The stench was stronger now, and I saw an Irish Catholic church just two streets away. I knew people had actually been worried about this particular structure being torched, as had been done to others during the religious riots in Pennsylvania. But the place was quiet, with several old women sitting in the front pews, and oddly, the scent of decay that had permeated the air outside so strongly had evaporated. There was no odor of anything besides candles and incense burning at the altar.

I slunk into a back pew and regarded the rose oculus window. The scene depicted a grieving Mother Mary in lapis lazuli blue as the sun, a bloody garnet, rose behind her. I closed my eyes and thought, hard. Why had Lucius thrown me off his scent? Was I wrong to assume that he wanted to bait me, so I could arrive at the correct church just as he put the match to the powder keg? What church would he choose—and why?

Then it hit me: I was being stupid. The vampire had done due diligence and found out exactly where my bride's family lived; he wouldn't have just chosen a random church to burn down. *He would have picked the chapel in which I was married.*

I knew the truth of this deep in my bones. But just as surely I knew that I couldn't go after him by myself. And there was only one person who was capable of helping me.

Damon.

Damon, who had trapped me into the stupid marriage that got the Sutherlands all killed. Damon, who had killed Callie. Damon, who swore to make my life a living hell for all eternity. But in the end I needed him. I had seen him control his powers in ways I could not. And I would need all the Power I could get on my side if I was to find a way to defeat an old one. Lexi had rescued us from prison, and surely even someone as debased and fallen as Damon would recognize that we owed her.

The only problem was finding him.

And now, I think I'm ready for a drink was what he had said. For most vampires that only meant one thing. For my brother, well, he could easily have meant hitting the bottle as well as draining a person or two. But where?

In the weeks between following me to New York and "finding" me at the Chesters' ball, he had, as Lexi said, been sweeping the New York society scene as an Italian count. He had probably talked—or compelled—his way into any number of private clubs or restaurants. I wracked my brains, trying to remember the prattle Bridget had bored me with, about who was seen where with whom, and where was the latest place to go, and how there was an oyster bar serving genuine Pimm's Cup, just like in England. For lack of any better idea, I went there first.

It was a lovely place in an otherwise unwholesome area at the southern seaport. Uncertain-looking sailors wandered from pool of streetlight to pool of streetlight, gathering in twos and threes to quietly discuss the seedier side of import and export, laugh loudly, and sing old drinking songs. Among all of this rotting seaweed, though, fancy livery and decorated carriages were parked: society men lured by the oysters, Pimm's Cups, and the dangerous aspect of the place.

Inside there were quite a few of the young men I had seen at the Chesters' ball, as well as at my own wedding. Even Bram was there, but he was keeping to himself and looked ill. His face was ashen and his eyes sunken, and he wore black ribbons around his sleeves for mourning. His drink was untouched and he just stared sadly out the windows at the river.

I turned my back to him, not wanting him to call out that a murderer—as he no doubt thought I was—was in their midst.

I beckoned for the hostess to come over.

"Has D—uh, the Count DeSangue been by here tonight?" I asked.

The girl looked me up and down, face flushing with excitement. "With him accused of murder and this being his favorite place and me being his favorite girl, what on earth would make me tell you something like that?"

I could see by the thick scarf she wore around her neck that she wasn't just warding off the cold night air—this had definitely been one of Damon's haunts.

I started to reach into my pocket for bribe money. She saw where I was going and shook her head. "Not on your life, love. Not for Damon."

"You have no idea who he is, or what you're getting involved in," I growled, grabbing her wrist. Her face fell and she tried to struggle out of my grasp. "*Listen to me.* I'm Stefan Salvatore—the other man accused of murdering the Sutherlands. Neither one of us did it, all right? We're *both* on the run from the police. *Now tell me where he is.*"

I didn't compel her. I didn't *exactly* threaten her. But she nodded mutely and I relaxed my grip.

"I don't know," she said, rubbing her wrist. "I know he liked a drink at some of those fancy uptown places like the

Skinny Black Cat and Xerxes' Repose. He even had his own table at the Twenty-Two Club."

At that moment a waitress came out. "Are you talking about the count?" she asked, an excited grin spreading across her face.

I sighed. "Yes."

"Well, he once took me to Strange Fruit just a few blocks down."

"He took you on a *date*?" the hostess said, envy apparent in her voice. The waitress nodded proudly.

"Thank you," I said, meaning it. Lexi or Damon would have compelled the women to forget me at that point. I sighed, thinking about how much easier life would be if my Powers were stronger and my will weaker.

I checked Winfield's pocket watch. It was five A.M.; an hour had passed since Lexi and I had first entered the mansion. Time was ticking by far too quickly for my liking, and every minute seemed to seal Lexi's fate more completely.

Seconds later I was standing inside the door of Strange Fruit, a large, low, dark bar with giant wooden fans slowly turning overhead. The sailors who couldn't get into the oyster bar were there, along with every type of shady personality, lost soul, and criminal genius that managed to stay just this side of the law.

Damon sat at a small rickety table by himself in just his

shirtsleeves, a half-empty bottle of bourbon before him.

"Nursing your wounds?" I asked, walking over. He didn't even bother looking surprised.

"A minor setback, brother. Don't forget I have those dowry checks. As soon as things quiet down a bit I, and they, are out of this town."

"Doubtful any bank would cash a check for a suspected murderer."

"You really need to stop thinking like a human and start thinking like a vampire. There is no bank teller I can't compel."

He stretched languorously and poured some drink into his glass. Then he offered the glass to me, and chugged a big swallow directly from the bottle.

"I need your help," I said, pushing the glass away. I handed him the piece of paper and filled him in on what had happened.

He squinted his eyes as he read it. "So?"

I looked at him, gape-mouthed.

"*He has Lexi,*" I repeated. Then, afraid he was too drunk to understand what that meant, I pointed out the obvious. "We have to save her!"

"Mm." He thought about it for a moment. "Nope."

He made a big show of slowly kicking his legs back up onto the table, as if he had been in the midst of an important activity when I had interrupted him.

"What is *wrong* with you?" I demanded. "You saw him—he'll destroy her!"

"So what?" Damon asked. "It was her choice to come to New York. No one asked her to come up here."

"She got us out of prison—"

"*We*, excuse me, *I* was doing, just fine in that department. You forget. We could have gotten out on our own. We didn't need her for that. She was meddling. If further meddling got her captured, well, that's her own damn fault."

The anger that had ignited in me upon finding the note from the beast was now stoked into a rage that almost had me turning into full vampire mode. For just a moment, I didn't care who saw me.

"You," I said, trying to calm down, trying to put the blackness I felt into words. Damon sat up and looked me in the eye almost eagerly, waiting for the fight.

"You are . . . you are . . ." I spat.

"I am what you made me," Damon said dully, lifting his glass as though to toast me.

I grabbed his shoulders. "No. You don't have to be a heartless killer. Even Katherine wasn't that."

Damon's eyes flashed. "Don't speak to me about who Katherine was! I knew her better than you did."

I shook my head. "Even you know that's not true. You loved her more, but I knew her just as well. All Katherine wanted was for the three of us to be together forever. She would not have wanted us to be at odds, fighting. She would not have wanted *this*."

The surprise and anger on his face at what I'd said was almost worth it. Almost. "I'm going to save Lexi. Or die trying. And if by some miracle I don't die—*I never want to see you again*."

And before he could prepare some witty comeback or some threat, I banged my way out into the night, leaving my brother behind forever.

25

Anger was all I had left, and I let rage fuel me the way human blood had in my first weeks as a vampire. I couldn't believe Damon's indifference, couldn't understand who he'd become. But him not helping didn't change what I needed to do: save Lexi.

Across the street a gentleman upon a coal-black mare was talking amiably down to a shopkeeper. The moment the shopkeeper went in to get something I grabbed the horse's reins and, breaking my vow for the second time in twenty-four hours, I compelled the rider to dismount and enjoy a nice long *walk* back home.

Though normally I'd be faster than a horse, I was hungry and drained, so with gentle whispers and a crack of the reins I was off uptown, loudly galloping upon the New York City streets. She was a fine beast and responded to my every gentle nudge, the slightest clench of my knees. With the wind in my hair and the leather in my grip, I almost felt like my old self again.

But the sky was beginning to lighten, in that hushed crystal blue of early morning, and I had to urge every last bit of speed out of the horse. Lexi's life might depend on it.

As we mounted the long drive up to the Richards' and took the small path to the family chapel on the right, I knew I had made the right decision. I could smell the old one's presence, the miasma of old blood, death, and decay that followed around him like a shadow. My horse whinnied in terror.

I leaped off the horse before she had really stopped and gave her a gentle spank. "Go home," I ordered. She reared up, as if unwilling to give up her newfound freedom, then turned and galloped away.

I ran into the great hall where I was wed, pushing aside a lone servant who stood in my way.

Lexi was there, tied to the altar like an ancient sacrifice. The smell of vervain burned my nose—her ropes had clearly been soaked in it. The sun had risen, and its presence came in the form of a bloodred puddle from an east-facing stained glass window. As the light slowly moved toward her feet she squirmed and gasped, trying to pull her legs out of the way. A wisp of smoke rose up where the deadly sun had just begun to touch her toes, and the strange smell of burning flesh filled the room.

"Lexi!" I yelled.

"Stefan!" she sobbed in pain and relief.

I thought fast. It would take me far too long to figure out how to remove the vervain-soaked ropes, and there was nothing I could cover the windows with, no tapestries or easily pulled-up rugs or runners. Without thinking of my own safety, I ran over and grabbed her small white hand, slipping my ring over her finger.

"But, Stefan," Lexi protested.

"You need it if you're going to keep chasing after and saving me," I said, pulling all her ropes off. The vervain burned my fingers raw, but preserved her until she was free. Despite the pain in my fingers, I felt light and hopeful. I had done it. I'd saved Lexi. "Now let's get you—"

But at that moment, a vervain-soaked net fell on us both, searing every inch of my body.

"Run!" I shouted, pushing Lexi out of the way.

She rolled to the floor, then reached for the edge of a pew to help right herself. As she extended her arm, though, it passed through a shaft of sunlight. Her eyes widened in wonder, clearly shocked that no smoke appeared and her skin didn't burn. And then she disappeared, blurring with vampire speed away from the scene.

I put up my hands, trying to keep the netting off my

face, but I twisted and cried out wherever the poisoned rope touched me.

The ancient vampire appeared, giant leather gloves on his hands and a big grin on his pale face.

"Hello." The corners of his mouth pulled back too far, revealing a set of strong white teeth wedged in decaying gums. "So predictable, coming to rescue a damsel in distress."

That foul odor of a slaughterhouse enveloped me like a hot wind in August: inescapable, absolute, and horrible. Despite the burning nets, I tried to turn away from it.

That only made him chuckle.

"Where is the one who is always near you and just out of your grasp, like a shadow? Where is your brother?"

I clenched my jaw. Knowing Damon, he was swilling his third whiskey, preparing to feast on a saloon girl or two.

Lucius studied my silent face, seeming to mistake it for bravado. "Well, it is no matter. I will get him eventually. Your brother is more like a real *vampyr* than you, no interest in anything outside his little world, no desire to do good. He may survive for a trifle longer."

"What do you plan to do with me?" I demanded. Though in truth, now that Lexi was safe, I didn't fear for my own safety. I wished only to have the chance to kill the monster, to stop him from exacting further revenge and preying on more humans.

But the vervain was drawing out my Power like a siphon, and I knew even scratching the old one would be a small victory.

The beast grabbed the net and threw me over his shoulder like I was nothing more than a bag of mice or feathers.

"My plans are not particularly spectacular," he said as he lumbered down the church's aisle. There were still rose petals on the floor, I noted, drying away into thin scraps of nothing. The flowers in vases were wilted, everything left to wither after the murder of the brides.

"But they will be enduring. Vampires can survive a very, *very* long time. Without food. Slowly starving over the centuries and still not dying." The net shifted as he shrugged. "Well, eventually, perhaps. I've never seen it happen, but I suppose we'll find out."

He took a sudden left into the private chapel, stopping in front of a set of double doors—the crypt, I suddenly realized with mounting dread. Although the doors were solid, carved marble, Lucius had no problem throwing them open, dumping me out of the net, and tossing me into a tiny stone room, barely larger than the dozen coffins interred there.

For one brief moment, I relished the feel of the cool air rushing over my burned skin.

But then he let out a low growl. "When your hunger for blood eats you from the inside and makes you go mad, do not worry—I will be there, listening. Watching. And laughing."

My last sight was of the ancient standing, outlined in a bright halo of the living world, waving. Then he threw the doors closed with a slam that echoed to the very heavens, and I was in utter darkness.

I raced to the doors and threw my weight against them. They didn't even rattle. Trying to quell my rising hysteria, I took in the dank, musty room, searching for an opening, a secret exit, an out, even though a voice at the back of my mind screamed, "It's a crypt, Stefan! Death is the only way out!"

I wove through the maze of coffins and sarcophagi. Even in my panic I noticed the ornate carvings and brass hinges. One of the marble tombs had the portrait of a young girl engraved in high relief. She had wide eyes and bow-shaped lips. I slumped over the carving, as though I could hug the girl resting beneath it.

At least Lexi was safe, I told myself. If nothing else, at least I could spend the centuries knowing that she was out there somewhere, living her life—protected by my ring. And maybe, just maybe, trying to find me.

"*So long*," I whispered to Lexi in the silence of the tomb.

As if on cue, the doors to the crypt opened one last time, and a petite blonde came hurtling through, landing with a thud at my feet.

"Lexi!" I cried as the doors slammed shut behind her, plunging us into darkness again.

"Hey there," she said weakly. "Fancy meeting you here."

26

"**W**hat are you *doing* here?" I demanded.

Lexi raised a brow at me. "Same thing you are. Looking forward to a long, painful eternity together."

"No, I mean why didn't you run?" I asked, resisting the urge to take her by the shoulders and shake her.

"Of course I ran, you idiot!" she snapped. "But I guess he expected I would. . . . I never even saw him come after me." I could feel her shiver in the dark. "He appeared out of nowhere." Her voice grew grim. "I wonder if that's how humans feel when they meet us. If we ever get out of this, I swear I am going to be nicer to them in the future. Humans, I mean. That vampire—now *him* I want to kill."

I put my hand on her forearm, softening. "I just pray we get that chance."

"Come, let's get out of here." She turned and swung her leg, putting the heel of her boot smack into the middle of the doors.

There was a resounding thud, but nothing budged.

She delivered another roundhouse kick to the doors. And another. And another.

Again, nothing happened.

"Together!" she insisted. On the count of three we both kicked.

"Maybe there's vervain in the stone . . . ?" I suggested.

Lexi looked grim. "Vervain doesn't make things indestructible. But there are other things that can be done to lock something up. Permanently. What about the walls?"

For the next hour we ran our fingers over the white walls, ceilings, and floors, our highly sensitive skin picking out even the most minute gaps. We ripped open sarcophagi, ransacked the corpses for tools.

"No knives, no diamond crosses, no silver-plate Bibles, no pennies for Charon, no lucky stone, no *nothing*," I growled, throwing my hands up in frustration.

"This doesn't look good," was all Lexi said.

Twenty-four hours later there was a service in the chapel. We could hear it with our Powers. It was a memorial to the Sutherlands, to the two brides who were killed, to the proud parents . . . along with a biting invective against the young men who did it, running off with the dowry money. Murderers, thugs, con men, robbers . . .

The only accusation that didn't make the list was "demon."

But none of the insults stopped us from screaming.

"Help!" I yelled. "In here! We're in here!"

Lexi added her voice to mine, screeching in different high-pitched tones that nearly blew out my eardrums. At one point I could hear a hollow-voiced Hilda whisper, "Do you hear something?" And our hopes were raised.

And then nothing. The service ended, people filed out, and once again we were completely, utterly alone.

With sigh, Lexi gave me my ring back.

"Many thanks for its loan," she said quietly, slipping it on my finger. "But I don't think it will do me—or you— much good now."

I hugged her tight. "Don't give up yet," I whispered in her ear.

But the words echoed hollowly within the crypt, having nowhere else to go.

27

There was nothing to indicate the passage of hours inside the windowless vault—not the barest suggestion of sunlight ever made its way under its doors. Days melted into weeks, maybe months. It felt as if an eternity had passed, and yet another stretched out endlessly before us.

Lexi and I had stopped talking. Not out of anger or hopelessness, but just because we couldn't anymore. We didn't have enough strength to force ourselves to scream when we heard someone approach, much less get up and fight the stone that kept us buried. There was no more strength to fight the darkness, no strength to stand up. If I'd still required my heart to survive, I'm not sure I'd have had the strength to keep blood pumping through my veins.

We lay silently next to each other. If anyone ever found

us, a hundred years from then, we would look pathetic, like a sister and brother in some horrible fairy tale trapped in a witch's basement.

Each passing second drained me of my Power. My eyes no longer parsed the darkness. The silence was absolute as sounds from the outside world faded into oblivion. All that I had left was my sense of touch—the feel of Lexi's waxy hand, the rough wood of the battered coffin next to me, the cool metal band of my useless ring.

I felt almost human again, in the worst possible way. And as my Power retreated painfully, so with it went my immortality. I had never noticed its continual presence until it began to disappear, leaving meat and bone, brain and fluids, and taking away all that was supernatural about me with it.

Except for my hunger.

My vampire side reacted to starvation. My teeth ached and burned with need so badly that I would have shed tears if I'd had any. Blood weaseled its way into my every thought. I dreamed of how it had beaded up, jewel-like, on Callie's finger when she'd cut herself. How smoky my childhood crush, Clementine Haverford, had tasted going down. How, as my father lay dying on the floor of his study, his blood had spread out around him like greedy, searching fingers, staining everything in sight a dark, delicious red.

In the end, everything comes back to blood. Vampires are nothing but hunger personified, designed expressly for the purpose of stealing blood from our victims. Our eyes compel them to trust us, our fangs rip open their veins, and our mouths drain them of their very life source.

Blood . . .

Blood . . .

Blood . . .

Blood . . .

The word whispered to me over and over, like a song caught in one's head, filling every crevice of my brain and coating each memory with its tantalizing scent.

And then a very familiar voice began to talk to me.

"Hello, Stefan."

"Katherine?" I croaked, barely able to get the words out.

I managed to turn my head just enough to see her sprawled voluptuously on a set of silk pillow cushions. She looked exactly as she had the night of the massacre, before they took her away and killed her. Beautiful and partially undressed, her pouty lips giving me a knowing smile.

"Are you . . . alive?"

"Shhhh," she said, leaning over to stroke my cheek. "You don't look well."

I closed my eyes as her intoxicating scent of lemon and ginger swept over me, so familiar and so real that I swooned. She must have fed recently because the heat from her skin burned in the cold tomb.

"I wish I could help you," she whispered, her lips close to mine.

"Your. Fault," I managed to breathe.

"Oh, Stefan," she scolded. "You may not have been as willing as your brother, but you didn't precisely *object* to my . . . ministrations."

As if to emphasize her words, she leaned over and pressed her soft lips to my cheek. Again . . . and again . . . dragging them down my parched neck. Very, very delicately, she teased me, letting the tips of her fangs just puncture my skin.

I moaned. My head spun.

"But. You. Burned," I rasped. "I saw the church."

"Do you wish me dead?" she asked, fire in her eyes. "Do you want me to burn, to collapse to the ground in a pile of ashes, simply because you can't have me all to yourself?"

"No!" I protested, trying to push her off my neck. "Because you made me a monster . . ."

Her laugh was light and melodic, like the wind chimes Mother had hung on the front porch of Veritas. "Monster? Really, Stefan, one day you will remember what you knew to be true back in New Orleans—that what I have given you is a gift, not a curse."

"You're as mad . . . as . . . Klaus. . . ."

She sat back, alarm etching lines around her amber eyes. Her lower lip wobbled. "How do you know about K—? "

The crypt doors exploded into a thousand shards of stone and wood, as though shot through with a cannon.

I covered my face, the light burning my eyes like acid. When I opened them again, Katherine was gone, and a blurry figure garbed in black wavered in the jagged doorway, haloed by the punishing light.

"Klaus?" Lexi whispered in a terrified voice, clutching my hand.

"Sorry to disappoint," came a wry voice.

"Damon!" I struggled to sit up.

"Stefan, don't you think it's time you stopped just waiting around for your big brother to come and rescue you?"

Without ceremony he reached in, grabbed my wrist, and flung me out of the crypt. I flew into the opposite wall and fell down into a heap on the marble floor. Damon was gentler with Lexi, though not by much. Another weightless corpse, she flopped against me, legs askew.

Dust and shrapnel floated around us like fog. I blinked at the nondescript walls, trying to get my bearings.

"Here," Damon said, holding out a silver flask. "You're going to need it to escape."

I put my lips against the mouth of the vessel. Blood. Sweet, sweet, blood . . .

A voice in the back of my mind shouted that it was *human* blood, but I silenced it with a splash of heady liquid. I drank deeply, desperately, groaning when Damon grabbed the flask away from me.

"Save some for the lady," he said.

Lexi drank greedily as well. Blood dripped down her chin and around her lips as she sucked hard and silently. Her skin, which had been drawn, pale and wrinkled as an old woman's, filled out and became pink and puffy.

"Thanks, sailor," she breathed. "I needed that."

Like a lamp filling a cellar with heat and light, I felt my own Power radiate through my limbs, returning my senses to what they were, imbuing my body with strength that I hadn't experienced since before I started eating only animals.

As my vision cleared, I gasped. Behind Damon, a black-haired woman stood with one hand to her temple, the other gripped into a fist at her side. Her eyes were closed and her body shook with the slightest of tremors. It looked like she was in deep pain, being held in place while unknown tortures were applied to her mind and body.

Margaret.

And she wasn't alone. There was a prone figure in front of her, writhing in pain, and I realized with a jolt that Margaret wasn't being tortured—she was the one inflicting pain in another. In *Lucius*.

In the super-vampire, so Powerful, yet still only a foot soldier of Klaus, the demon directly descended from hell. Lucius had murdered an entire family, captured me with ease, and caught Lexi like a troublesome mouse. The monster had his head in his hands and was screaming, terrible screams that seemed to send reverberations through the very chapel.

"Is that *Margaret*?" I asked, dumbfounded.

Damon pulled me up, propelled me toward the door.

"We can't leave her!"

"She'll be fine!"

"But—"

"Questions later. Running *now*."

And so, with one last look at the woman who had brought Hell itself to its knees, I ran away from the site of my imprisonment and out into moonlight.

28

The three of us tore out of the chapel. As soon as we left the Richards' estate grounds we were plunging through woods. Saplings stung our legs as we pitched downhill through the wet night, and tall pines blocked whatever moonlight might have slipped between the clouds. If we had been human, our feet would have surely skidded on the forest floor of decaying leaves. Unable to see more than a yard or so in front of us we would have crashed into the giant trunk of a tree.

Instead, we moved like predators, coursing through the night like vampires had for hundreds of years: streaking through the wilds to the next village of potential victims, chasing down someone who had foolishly separated from the herd and decided to travel at night by himself.

It felt good to be racing this way, with a few ounces of

human blood zinging through my veins. I was almost able to lose myself in the flight, forgetting about what it was we were fleeing from.

Then there was a noise.

It started out like the beginning of a long roll of thunder, climbed into a crescendo of inhuman groaning, and ended in a screech of despair. The noise was everywhere, filling our ears, the valley we were descending into, the sky above us.

The three of us stopped, startled by the sound.

"Well, I guess the vampire is free," Damon huffed.

"Margaret—" I began.

"Trust me, she's fine. Did you see what she did to him?" Damon pointed out.

"What is she, though?" I asked.

"A witch."

"Like Emily?" I wondered, my theory confirmed. Was the world simply full of witches, vampires, demons, and who knows what else, most of which were invisible to human eyes?

"I had a feeling there was something different about her when I couldn't compel her . . ." Damon explained. "So I asked. And she answered. Pretty straightforward, that one."

"So she . . ."

"Cast a protective spell around herself and her family,

and was burning his brain meats with some mental abil-ity or other to buy us a little time. Emphasis on the word *little*," he added. "Hope that protective spell is still up."

There was another roar.

"Keep moving," Lexi ordered, and we began again.

The woods grew blacker as if nature herself dreaded his approach, and we could feel the earth tremble with his every footstep.

Damon and I leaped over a giant log, and for one fleet-ing moment our motions were perfectly synchronized. But then the three of us came to skidding halt at the edge of a cliff that looked out over all of upper Manhattan.

"Huh," my brother said doubtfully, peering over its edge.

"We'll have to find some other way down," I said, start-ing to look back the way we came. "A path, or . . ."

With a cry, Lexi hurled herself over the edge of the cliff.

I watched her, wide-eyed with horror.

"*Find another way down?*" Damon said, shaking his head disappointedly at me. "Still thinking like a human, brother." And he dove after her.

I swore under my breath, watching him disappear into the branches below. Then I followed.

As frightening as that fall was, there was something very freeing about it. I was weightless, swimming through the air. The world whistled through my outstretched fingers and hair. It almost felt as though I were flying.

I smashed down through thick leafy canopy and rolled into a ball, eventually coming right side up with a twisted ankle that reset itself almost before I noticed it.

Damon and Lexi were standing still. She had her head cocked, listening to the strange quiet we suddenly found ourselves in.

"He lost us," Damon said, triumphantly. "He didn't realize we went down the cliff! He's . . ."

"He's in front of us," Lexi breathed, eyes widening. The silence to the south was in fact complete, as if every living thing had quieted or died. We waited, unsure what to do, though it was hard to say for what.

Then came the sound of a single blade of grass bending and breaking.

"*RUN!*" Lexi screamed.

We took off. I made the mistake of looking behind me. What I saw and what I heard didn't match up; on the one hand, it briefly appeared that an older man was following me with surprising swiftness. But the shadow cast by the moonlight was of something far bigger and inhumanly shaped. Bushes and trees fell and crashed out of his way before he even touched them.

I doubled my pace.

We had no choice but to head south. The woods

thinned and civilization began to rear its ugly head: a lonely, last farm, a cluster of abandoned holdings, a large estate, a hotel, dirt roads to paved avenues still crowded with horses and carriages and cabs and people even in the middle of this night.

And behind us, gaining power from every shadow through which he passed, was the old one.

We turned a corner around a fruit stand, knocking down baskets, and the stench of decay that issued from his raggedy breathing mouth was hot on my neck. We dashed through a slum, avoiding clotheslines and open pits of raw sewage, and he was there, throwing aside things and people to get to us. When we thought we had pulled ahead, twisting through narrow alleys and confusing side streets, we could still feel his Power, his frustration vibrating through the night.

Lexi led us, and whether it was her own Power or a familiarity with the city, she managed to find just the right fire escapes to leap to, just the right piles of garbage to roll over. Perhaps this was not the first time she had fled from a demon of this stature.

"The seaport," she hissed. "It's our only chance."

Damon nodded, for once having no trouble taking orders from someone else. We made our way to the west, to the avenues bordering the mighty Hudson.

Lexi's eyes suddenly narrowed and she pointed. A

clipper ship, a pretty shiny blue vessel just pulling away from the dock, filled with all sorts of New York goods to sell overseas.

With a mighty leap Lexi cleared the water between the dock and its deck, arms poised in the air like a cat leaping upon its prey. Damon and I followed suit, silently landing on the dark deck. By the time we recovered ourselves she was already compelling a shocked sailor who had seen the manner of our arrival.

"We're on the manifest. My brothers and I have a berth below. We did not just leap aboard. . . ."

Damon surveyed the ship with interest, pleased with his new locale.

I looked back toward shore. There stood a single, innocuous-seeming man leaning against the rail of the wharf, pale as if he had sucked all the moonlight into himself. He stood casually, like he was just there to watch the ships come and go.

But the look in his eyes was deadly and eternal—and unforgiving.

er name was the *Mina M.* She was a speedy ship and a thing of beauty, with sleek lines and white sails. Her wooden mast was oiled to a sheen, boasting smart red flags that snapped in the breeze.

I stood at the prow and closed my eyes, imagining our journey. The stinging salt air and the bright yellow sun would whip my cheeks red as the *Mina* cut through waves, leaving white foam and spray in her wake. Little silver fish would glint in the water below in their hurry to get out of the way.

On our travels we would see tiny skiffs cross the water loaded up with bananas and rum in the West Indies. We'd trade for spices in India. I'd finally see Italy, walk through the Sistine Chapel, marvel in front of the Duomo, and drink Chianti straight from the vineyard.

Maybe . . . maybe this would be a new way of life for me. Traveling at the speed of water rather than confining myself to the shadows. I'd never stay in one port for too long, outrunning death and my curse. Sailors usually had no friends but the men they crewed with—I would fit right in.

But then I opened my eyes, my fantasy evaporating into the heavy midnight that surrounded me. A dense cloud cover obscured the sky and any stars embedded there failed to shine through. The *Mina* slipped silently out to sea, cutting the oily water with barely a hiss.

This was the vampire's realm. Though my ring allowed me to walk in the daylight, my world existed in darkness. It was then, while the sun slumbered, that I hunted, evaded enemies, spewed curses, broke promises, and gave myself over to hate. We had escaped Klaus's minion, but we hadn't defeated him. He and his master were still out there, somewhere, planning on future torture and death for me and Damon.

Lexi came up on deck behind me and touched my shoulder.

"We're en route to San Francisco," she said quietly. "I've not been there . . . in a while. But you'll love the fog and dismal weather. *Great* for brooding." She gave me a thin smile. "And I can tell you're going to be quite the brooder."

I leaned against the deck rail. I didn't have the heart to tell her that there would never be a place for me, that I would never fit. And I didn't deserve to, after all the lives I'd ended.

The night wind tousled my thick brown hair and Lexi tucked it behind my ear.

"He said *an eye for an eye*," I began.

"Yes. Well." Lexi took a deep sigh and looked serious for a moment, eyes narrowing. "This is a fast ship and it will take him time to figure out our manifest. Besides the legal cargo of tea and coffee, there's a sizable shipment of opium they're planning to pick up in Frisco. The captain failed to register with the dock master, so it will be a while before anyone figures out where we turn tail to."

"No. I mean yes, that's good." I rubbed a sudden spray of water from my eyes. "But I meant . . . he killed the people that were supposed to be our wives, because his Katherine was killed."

Lexi nodded, shivering.

"And then he grabbed you . . . and was going to kill you and me, and probably Damon, in a church, just like Katherine was killed."

Lexi narrowed her eyes. "I'm not sure I understand where you're going with this."

"If he was being so particular about whom he killed and in what manner, *why didn't he set the place on fire?*"

Lexi blinked. I saw her work through the logic. She stayed silent for a long time. I couldn't read her eyes, but still I felt embarrassed to be thinking of Katherine at a time like this.

"Stefan," she began. "Please listen to me. There are all levels of evil among our kind. From that old thing that commits great atrocities to . . . minor, horrible little things that exist just for their own pleasure, regardless of whom it hurts.

"Katherine wanted you to become a vampire. And look at the results. Do not weep overmuch for her, Stefan, or search for clues to her death or existence. *Let her go.* It is truly the best thing you can do."

I turned my head away from her and looked toward the only star bright enough to shine through the cloud cover—the North Star. Katherine was like that star: fixed in place, a silent specter hanging above me, a benchmark against which to measure my progress. No matter my feelings toward her, she had made me, and she would be with me always.

"We're not *all* evil," I said, putting my arm around her. "You're not."

"I'm a lot older than you," she said gently. "And who I am now isn't who I've always been. You're not the only one with things to atone for, Stefan. But I've made a vow to myself to be different."

"Oh, *ugh. Vows.*" Damon stumbled onto deck loudly. "By

Our Lord, haven't we made enough vows for a lifetime?"

"The marriages were your idea, not mine," I pointed out.

"Waah, wahh, I'm a vampire, I had a really great wedding, great champagne, my brother rescued me, and I'm still tortured."

He bounced off the deck rails, palming the smooth wood and propelling himself back to the other side, port to starboard back and forth until he reached us. The untrained eye would have marked him as drunk, but there was a telltale crimson smear in the corner of his lips. He was drunk with our escape, with our rescue, with the lifeblood of some poor cabin boy—but not with drink. Not yet, at least.

"Yes, and speaking of rescues, Margaret . . ." I prompted.

Damon sighed. "When I confronted her about being able to withstand compulsion, Margaret admitted she was a witch and said she would help me."

"Just like that?" I asked skeptically.

Damon rolled his eyes. "In return for us leaving New York and never coming back—in her lifetime, at least. And, this is the part that kills me, *returning the dowries*."

"Aw, Damon. I'm so sorry," Lexi said, her sparkling eyes belying her serious tone. "Your plan to fleece the rich didn't work out. Better luck next time." She punched him lightly in the shoulder.

"We owe her our lives," I said seriously. "She didn't

have to help us at all. By all rights, she *shouldn't* have. The protection spell she cast around her and her husband—do you think it will really keep them safe?"

"I have to believe. Either way, she's a better soul than you lot," Lexi pronounced.

"And speaking of better souls . . ." I said, barely suppressing a smile, "what made you come back and rescue me? I thought you were hell-bent on 'never forgiving me' and 'punishing me until the end of my days.'"

Damon's blue eyes were veiled. "Yes. Well, I meant every word. I will *never* forgive you. I *will* torture your every living moment."

I shook my head, tamping down the stirring of black rage inside me that wanted to shout to Damon that he may have lost the love of his life, but I lost a life that I loved. And a father, and a home.

And a brother.

But as quickly as the rage flowed in, it ebbed back out again, leaving me hollow. How could I expect my brother to forgive me for turning him into a vampire when I couldn't forgive myself for it? He had once loved me, as I had once loved Katherine, but I would never, ever forgive her for making me what I was now.

Damon took me by the shoulders. "Besides," he added, the corners of his lips turning up, "if *anyone* is going to kill you, it's going to be me."

Then, without another word, he leaped with vampiric speed to the deck rail itself, balancing without moving a muscle as the boat dipped and rocked in the water, as though he were the ship's figurehead, carved in cold marble.

He lifted his hand in salute. "I'll be seeing you, brother."

Then, before I could even utter his name, he stepped off the rail and plunged into the dark water below.

I raced to the edge of the boat and looked at the churning water. But my brother didn't resurface. Lexi and I stood there for what felt like an eternity, until we were so far from shore and sky that it felt as though we were suspended in blackness.

Then, when the sun finally peeked its red head over the watery horizon, we went inside the dimly lit cabin to face our future.

My time in New York clarified the perils of my existence; despite my good intentions, I am dangerous to humans, and my brother is dangerous to everyone.

And now? What does the future hold? My days seem to pass like minutes. I suppose this means I'm growing accustomed to the idea of eternity.

I have lost so much in the months since I became the creature I now am. But I have gained time. And with time, I gain opportunity. I will see Italy. And the rest of Europe. I will travel the whole world. But I will never make a home among humans again.

As for Damon . . . I believe our road together is long and our story is not over yet. Should one of us ever finally come *to his doom, it will only be the other who causes it.*

And in the background . . . heralded by the faint perfume of lemon and ginger . . . will always be Katherine, laughing at both of us.

Don't miss the new Vampire Diaries trilogy,

The Hunters

Read an exclusive sneak peek
of the first volume, *Phantom*!

Elena Gilbert stepped onto a smooth expanse of grass, the spongy blades collapsing beneath her feet. Clusters of scarlet roses and violet delphiniums pushed up from the ground while a giant canopy hung above her, twinkling with glowing lanterns. On the terrace in front of her stood two curving white marble fountains that shot sprays of water high into the air. Everything was beautiful, and elegant, and somehow familiar.

This is Bloddeuwedd's palace, a voice in her head said. But when she had been here last, the field had been crowded with laughing, dancing partygoers. They were gone now, though signs of their presence remained: empty glasses littering the tables set around the edges of the lawn, a silken shawl tossed over a chair, a lone high-heeled shoe perched on the edge of a fountain.

2 ◆ *The Vampire Diaries*

Something else was odd, too. Before, the scene had been lit by the hellish red light that illuminated everything in the Dark Dimension, turning blues to purples, whites to pinks, and pinks to the velvety color of blood. Now a clear white light shone over everything, and a full white moon sailed calmly overhead.

A whisper of movement came from behind her, and Elena realized with a start that she wasn't alone after all. A dark figure was suddenly *there*, approaching her.

Damon.

Of course it was Damon, Elena thought with a smile. If anyone was going to appear unexpectedly before her, here, at what felt like the end of the world—or at least the hour after a good party had ended—it would be Damon. God, he was so beautiful. Black on black: soft black hair, eyes black as midnight, black jeans, and a smooth leather jacket.

As their eyes met, she was so glad to see him that she could hardly breathe. She threw herself into his embrace, clasping him around the neck. She felt the lithe, hard muscles in his arms and chest as he held her tight.

"Damon," she said, her voice trembling for some reason. Her body was trembling, too, and Damon stroked her arms and shoulders, calming her.

"What is it, princess? Don't tell me you're afraid." He smirked lazily at her, but his hands were strong and steady.

"I *am* afraid," she answered.

"But what are you afraid of?"

That left her puzzled for a moment. Then, slowly, putting her cheek against his, she said, "I'm afraid that this is just a dream."

"I'll tell you a secret," he said into her ear. "You and I are the only real things here. It's everything else that's the dream."

"Just you and I?" Elena echoed, an uneasy thought nagging at her, as though she was forgetting something—or someone. A fleck of ash landed on her dress, and she absently brushed it away.

"It's just the two of us, Elena," Damon said sharply. "You're mine. I'm yours. We've always loved each other, since the beginning of time."

Of course. That must be why she was trembling—it was joy. He was hers. She was his. They belonged together.

She whispered one word, "Yes."

Then he kissed her.

His lips were soft as silk, and when the kiss deepened, she tilted her head back, exposing her throat, anticipating the double wasp-sting he'd delivered so many times.

When it didn't come, she opened her eyes questioningly. The moon was bright as ever, and the scent of roses hung heavy in the air. But Damon's chiseled features were pale under his dark hair, and more ash had landed on the shoulders of his jacket. All at once, the little doubts that had been niggling at her came into clear focus.

Oh, no. Oh, *no*.

"Damon," she gasped, looking into his eyes despairingly as tears filled her own. "You can't be here, Damon. You're . . . dead."

"For more than five hundred years, princess." Damon flashed his blinding smile at her. "I don't know why it's such a shock to you."

More ash was falling around them, like a fine gray rain. Like the ash Damon's body was buried beneath, worlds and dimensions away.

"Damon, you're . . . dead now. Not undead, but . . . gone."

"*No*, Elena—"

"Yes. Yes! I held you as you died. . . ." Elena was sobbing helplessly. She couldn't feel Damon's arms at all now. He was disappearing into shimmering light.

"Listen to me, Elena—" She was holding moonlight. Anguish caught at her heart.

"All you need to do is call for me," Damon's voice said. "All you need . . ."

His voice faded into the sound of wind rustling through the trees. Elena's eyes snapped open. The room was full of sunlight, and a huge crow was perched on the sill of her open window. A cloud must have gone over the sun; for a moment, the world was dim.

The crow tilted its head to one side and gave another croak, watching her with bright eyes.

A cold chill ran down her spine. "Damon?" she whispered.

But the crow just spread its wings and flew away.

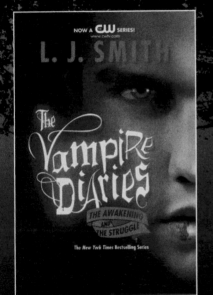
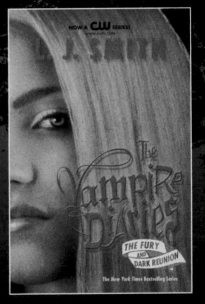 

A THRILLING TALE OF
LOVE, WITCHCRAFT, AND
THE SUPERNATURAL